WEST OF THE BAR 10

A group of mysterious riders is racing along the border of the infamous Bar 10 spread, determined to fulfil one mission — the killing of Johnny Puma. With his time running out, Johnny will need to rely on more than his wits if he is to face this pack of murderous strangers and survive. It's time to accept the help of his loyal friends — the famed and dangerous riders of the Bar 10.

Books by Boyd Cassidy
in the Linford Western Library:

BAR 10 JUSTICE
BAR 10 GUNSMOKE
GOLD OF THE BAR 10
DEATH RIDER
THE HOT SPURS

BOYD CASSIDY

WEST OF THE BAR 10

Complete and Unabridged

LINFORD
Leicester

First published in Great Britain in 2014 by
Robert Hale Limited
London

First Linford Edition
published 2016
by arrangement with
Robert Hale Limited
London

A catalogue record for this book is available
from the British Library.

ISBN 978–1–4448–2931–0

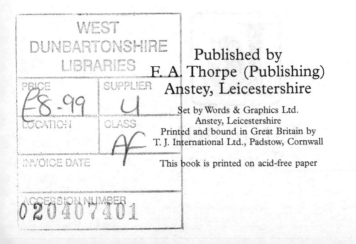

Published by
F. A. Thorpe (Publishing)
Anstey, Leicestershire

Set by Words & Graphics Ltd.
Anstey, Leicestershire
Printed and bound in Great Britain by
T. J. International Ltd., Padstow, Cornwall

This book is printed on acid-free paper

Dedicated to my cousin Nick George.
Keep cooking, cuzz.

Prologue

The famed Bar 10 cattle spread had many unanswered mysteries but one of the most intriguing concerned the young man who had become like a son to rancher Gene Lon Adams. Johnny Puma had yet to reach his thirtieth birthday and had spent more than a decade on the vast Texas ranch but even so he had never truly been a cowboy like those he worked with. Every inch of the young man told a different tale. The pair of matched Colt .45s in their hand-tooled shooting rig spoke of another life that had gone before his arrival at the legendary Bar 10 ranch.

A life which had been very different from that of the humble cowpuncher he purported to be. The speed and accuracy with which Johnny Puma could use his guns was something rare in cowboys. Most cowboys had never even fired their guns in anger, but tended to use them as a tool.

In total contrast Johnny Puma could not only use his guns but had proved his ability with them on numerous occasions. For him his guns were a vital part of his being. They had contributed to his survival and helped him protect those who surrounded him. Like Adams himself, he was a renowned shot and never spoke of how he had learned his often lethal skill.

It was well known amongst his fellow riders of the Bar 10 that Adams had given him the name he now used. The rancher had also given the youngster a new life and protected him as though Johnny were the son Adams had never been blessed with.

A score of theories as to why Johnny had needed a new identity had come and gone over the years, but Adams had never spoken of it. Only he and his ancient pal Tomahawk knew the truth and they were not telling.

There was an unwritten code at the

Bar 10. They were a family of strangers who had little but their own gritty courage and resolve to protect them. It was said that when you were accepted into the Bar 10 fold you remained for ever.

Gene Lon Adams would protect his cowboys whatever the cost. They were his sons and a real man was always willing to make the ultimate sacrifice for his children.

But sometimes fate moves its great hand and the past returns to haunt the present with a vengeance. Sometimes even men like Gene Adams cannot hold back the tide of a tempest no matter how hard he tries.

Sometimes even ten years is not long enough for all of the demons which linger in the shadows of a man's soul to be vanquished permanently.

There were indeed many mysteries on the Bar 10.

Johnny Puma was just one of them.

This past was riding towards the vast ranch with bloody spurs. Soon the youngster would have to face his demons and all those around him would learn the truth. Every question would be answered.

None of the riders of the Bar 10 knew it, but death was coming. The past was returning to haunt them.

1

The sandstorm was blinding as it swept in from the desolate prairie, across the vast grasslands and along the streets of Sutter's Corner. It was like a living creature more monstrous than any nightmare. A sheer wall of sand that nearly blotted out the sun continued to roll unchecked over everything in its path. The residents of the normally bustling town had taken refuge in the numerous stores and saloons to wait for the seasonal storm to subside. Yet the wind continued to whip up the fine sand as though the Devil himself wanted to conceal the arrival of his most black-hearted of disciples.

The dozen horsemen steered their way down the middle of the wide main street, through the choking cloud of sand. Not even the keenest of eyes saw the arrival of the most dangerous gang ever to have entered its unmarked boundaries, and there would have been little they could have done even if they had. Each of the horsemen had his bandanna raised up and the brim of his Stetson pulled down. Their cold-blooded eyes squinted against the biting sandstorm as each of the outlaws stared out ahead.

As always the outlaws were ready to kill anyone who even hinted at slowing their deadly progress. They were on a path of lethal retribution with only one thought filling their minds.

They had the scent of their prey in their nostrils. They knew that the man they sought was closer now than he had been for the previous decade. Even the storm of sand which tormented them and their horses could not deter them from the man they sought.

They had ridden a hundred miles to achieve their unholy goal and finish their slaughtering. To find and kill the one man who had managed to survive their vicious and brutal attack on a small settlement ten years earlier.

Most killers would have been satisfied with having made the lone survivor a man who was wanted dead or alive. They would have been happy that the innocent youngster had been branded with their crimes and forced to flee for his very life, but not the horsemen who steered their mounts deeper into the heart of Sutter's Corner.

They had unfinished business.

It would only be finished when blood was spilled.

His blood.

Nothing else would satisfy them.

For years they had not heard anything of Johnny Mason. He had somehow vanished and each of the brutal outlaws had assumed that he had fallen victim to a lawman's bullet or rope.

The gang had recalled the last time they had seen Mason, after he had been cornered by a posse. He had been covered in his own blood and carrying the lead of those who hunted him in his youthful body.

It had been easy to assume that he had died of his injuries all those years before. The gang had destroyed an entire town and its inhabitants and filled their pockets with each of the victims' loot. They had also managed to pin the blame on the innocent youngster to divert attention from themselves.

It had all worked perfectly.

Only the final piece of the jigsaw puzzle had eluded them and that had always been a thorn in their hides. They had wanted to make sure that Johnny Mason was dead but they had failed in the final part of their sickening scheme.

Weeks had become years. After so many other equally horrific crimes the memory of the wronged Mason had faded.

Then, ten days earlier, as the gang were enjoying the spoils of yet another successful bank robbery, a drunken man in a tobacco-smoke-filled saloon had told them that he had seen Johnny Mason only a month before. After the gang had poured even more whiskey into the old-timer they became convinced that he was telling the truth.

Johnny Mason was alive but, strangely, not answering to his name. Now he had another name. Now he was Johnny Puma and one of many cowboys working for the famed Bar 10 cattle ranch.

The drunken man swore that he was an old friend of the youngster and knew that he was not mistaken. He had seen and spoken to Johnny Mason.

Suddenly the memories of those long-gone days had returned to the gang. Normally they would not have bothered to resume their hunt for the man whom they had managed to turn into a wanted outlaw like themselves.

But Johnny Mason had been good with his guns and, unlike so many of their victims, he had fought back like a cornered tiger.

They wanted revenge.

There had once been eighteen members of the Savage gang and Johnny Mason had managed to kill six of them before he himself had become the hunted and no longer the hunter when the law was steered after him.

For years Bart Savage had thought that the youngster whom they had managed to get blamed for their hideous crimes must be dead. Now they knew that he was alive, and that burned in each of their craws.

Mason still lived.

That had to be rectified.

Bart Savage led his lethal followers silently through the sandstorm down the long street. They were like dust-caked ghosts. Every stride of his lathered-up mount reminded him that Johnny Mason had killed his three brothers after they in turn had murdered every other living soul in the distant town of Rio Maria. Two other members of his gang had also lost kin but that did not matter to Savage.

He wanted revenge.

Savage drew rein and raised a long leg over the cantle of his mount. His spurs rang out in the gloom as he leaned over the barely visible hitching rail and looped his long leathers over it. He tied his reins tightly.

One by one each of his followers replicated his actions and stepped away from their mounts to gather around their leader like a small army seeking a war to enter into.

The blinding sandstorm made it impossible for any of the gang to read the words painted on the long wooden boards above the porch but the smell of stale liquor was unmistakable. They had found a saloon and they were thirsty.

Their spurs rang out as one by one the outlaws stepped up on to the board-walk and moved to the swing doors. Savage led the way into the crowded saloon. The swing doors rocked on their hinges after the last of the gunmen had entered.

A hushed silence greeted them.

Twelve sand-covered men with their bandannas raised up over their noses was the last thing any of the saloon's patrons had expected to see. Savage tugged on his bandanna to reveal his scarred features. He walked across the sawdust-covered floor to the bar counter. His men moved to either side of him as the rest of the saloon's patrons spread wide and clear of the strangers.

'Whiskey, barkeep. A bottle apiece,' Savage drawled as he tossed a golden fifty-dollar coin at the nervous man who stood before a long mirror.

The bartender nodded. His shaking hands pulled black glass bottles from under the counter and set them down in front of each of the dust-caked outlaws.

'You boys looking for work?' the bartender asked. He moved to his cash register and started to withdraw Savage's change. 'I hear the Lazy M are taking on hands for the cattle drive.'

Savage raised the bottle to his mouth. His teeth pulled the cork from the bottle's neck. Savage spat it at the spittoon next to his boots.

'We're here looking for a long-lost friend,' Savage lied as he drank from his bottle. 'Maybe you know him?'

'What's his handle?' the bartender asked, placing the coins and bills before the outlaw leader. 'I know most of the cowpokes in these parts.'

'His name's Johnny,' Savage continued as his men began to down their fiery liquor around him. 'I'm told he rides a pinto pony nowadays.'

The bartender smiled. 'I surely do. There's only one critter that fits that description in these parts. You mean Johnny Puma. He rides for the Bar 10. Am I right?'

Savage nodded. 'That's him.'

The bartender rested his hands on the wet counter. 'The Bar 10 boys don't come into town much this close to a cattle drive. It would take something mighty important to bring them off the ranch.'

'Something important, huh?' Savage sucked on the neck of his bottle again, then placed it down on the counter. He looked thoughtful as his left hand went to his Remington and drew it from his holster. He cocked its hammer as his men smiled and the bartender backed off. He looked around the saloon at the faces of its other patrons until he saw a female huddled close to a few burly men.

He levelled the barrel of his gun at the bar-room girl.

'What you doing?' the bartender asked fearfully.

Savage squeezed his trigger. The deafening sound of the shot echoed around inside the saloon. The female fell into a heap in the midst of the crowd. Blood suddenly encircled her dead body. The blood-splattered patrons backed up to a wall and stared in disbelief at the stranger with the smoking six-shooter in his hand.

The cold-blooded eyes of the deadly outlaw glanced at the bartender and a cruel smile etched itself across his face.

'Get a horse and ride to the Bar 10. Tell Johnny that his old friend Bart Savage wants to talk with him,' Savage snarled at the shaking bartender. 'Tell him me and my boys will keep killing until he shows. Savvy?'

'I'll tell him.' The bartender removed his apron and walked round from the counter. He had barely reached the swing doors when he heard the gun firing again. He heard another body hit the sawdust-covered floor as he raced out into the sandstorm.

2

Sheriff Hardy Willis was a burly man who had a gut that hung over the buckle of his gunbelt. He had been up since just before daybreak and had wrongly imagined that the sandstorm would mean that Sutter's Corner would be quiet for another day. He stared at the blotter on his desk and the coffee that he had spilled when the first shot had echoed around the small community. When a second shot had erupted out in the street the lawman realized that something was wrong. It was quite common to hear shots in any town west of the Pecos as men celebrated their various vices, but years of experience as a lawman told Willis that this was different.

This was no drunken reveller trying to shoot crows out of the sky. Every instinct told Willis that the shots he had just heard had more than likely been deadly.

The sheriff rose from his chair and dried his hands on his vest front. Willis had barely reached the solitary window of the his weather-worn office when he caught a fleeting glimpse of a rider spurring hard past the Main Street office door. The sandstorm had hidden most of the horseman from the eyes of the rotund lawman but for a few confused seconds Willis had thought it had been Bob Charles, the bartender from the Longhorn saloon.

That confused him. He had never seen the bartender even close to a horse, let alone riding one.

Sheriff Willis gritted what was left of his teeth, raised an arm and plucked his hat from the stand near the door. There was a blizzard blowing outside the window and door of his small office.

A blizzard of sand.

It was finding every way it could to enter the office around the ill-fitting door. Sheriff Willis placed the hat on his balding head, secured its drawstring under his multitude of chins and tightened it.

He had battled against the storm to reach his office a few hours earlier and did not relish venturing out into it again, but men who wore tin stars often had to do the very thing their better judgement warned them against.

There was no let-up in the storm. In fact it seemed to Willis to be even worse than it had been at sunup. His whiskered features were still raw from his earlier walk through the brutal windblown sand. It had cut through his flesh like barbed wire.

Suddenly another shot rang out.

Willis jolted in surprise. A bead of sweat traced down his face. He was no coward, but he was not a man who ever went looking for trouble either. Something was happening out there beyond the blanket of sand and no matter how much he wanted to ignore it, he could not. Willis had been a lawman too long to do nothing. It was his job to protect the people who paid his salary. A million questions flashed through the sheriff's mind.

Only two of them managed to stick.

Who was shooting and who was being shot?

The lawman picked his topcoat off the wooden hook of the stand and slid it on. He had no sooner started to button it than he heard the sound of boots echoing on the boardwalk to his left. Someone was running towards his office.

Willis pushed his nose against the pane of glass just as a figure emerged from the sand and twisted the handle of his door. The sheriff stepped back and watched Joel Harker enter his office, closing the door behind him.

The lawman looked at the blacksmith long and hard. He had never seen the well-built man look so terrified before. It troubled him. When men like Harker were frightened there had to be something to be frightened of.

'What's wrong, Joel?' Willis asked as the man spat sand from his mouth and coughed. 'What's eating at you? Did you see who has been firing that gun?'

The muscular man straightened up. He was well over six feet in height but he was shaking with fear.

'Nope, I didn't see the critter that's firing that hogleg, Sheriff. But Bob sure did,' Harker managed to say. 'He told me about it when he hired one of my saddle horses.'

'So it was Bob I saw riding past here.' Willis nodded to himself. 'I've never seen him riding before. What did he tell you, Joel? What?'

'He said that a varmint called Savage gunned down Maisie Hooper in the saloon, Sheriff,' Harker replied in a croaking voice. He rested a hip on the desk and cupped his face in his massive hands. 'Bob said he heard him shoot someone else just as he left the Longhorn but Bob didn't look back. He started running and didn't stop until he reached my livery.'

Willis moved close to the shaking blacksmith.

'Savage?'

Harker nodded and looked straight into the eyes of the lawman. 'Yep, Bart Savage. He and about ten or more others rode in a short while back. Why'd he kill Maisie for, Sheriff? Bob said that Savage just killed her like she was nothing but a piece of meat.'

Willis moved to his desk and pulled open a drawer. He grabbed a two-inch pile of Wanted posters, set them down next to the blacksmith and started to thumb his way through them until he found the one he sought.

The one with the name of Bart Savage printed in bold black letters just above the words WANTED DEAD OR ALIVE.

'Holy smoke!' the sheriff gasped as he handed the poster to his friend and bit his lip. 'We've got us a real bad *hombre* in town, Joel.'

'It don't mention his gang here, Sheriff,' Harker said, as his large finger traced along the lettering. 'Just says he's a bank robber and worth two thousand dollars.'

The lawman shook his head. 'Where was Bob going on that rented horse in such a hurry, Joel?'

'Bob was going to the Bar 10,' the blacksmith replied. 'Savage sent him there to tell Johnny Puma he had to come to town.'

'What the hell for?' The sheriff looked totally confused and as troubled as the blacksmith beside him.

Harker inhaled deeply just as another shot rang out in the street. 'I got me a feeling that this Bart Savage wants to kill Johnny as well. Bob said that the varmint told him he was gonna keep killing folks until Johnny shows. It sounds like he meant it.'

The veteran lawman drew his .45 from its holster and checked it. When satisfied the weapon was fit for purpose he lowered it back into its holster.

The blacksmith looked at his friend. 'You ain't thinking of going up against that madman, are you?'

Without replying Willis walked to his gun rack and pulled a shotgun down. He then filled his jacket pockets with ammunition and turned to face the door again.

Harker stood and looked down at the shorter lawman. He could not disguise his concern.

'Are you? Are you gonna go up against a whole gang of gun-crazy killers, Hardy?' the blacksmith asked fearfully. 'That's suicide. They got no respect for ordinary folks and I'll bet you a new hat that men wearing tin stars don't live too long in their company.'

The sheriff paused for a moment as he cradled the scattergun and gripped the handle of his door. He looked at the blacksmith and forced a smile.

'It's what I'm paid to do, Joel.'

Before the blacksmith could say another word the lawman had opened the door and closed it behind him. Harker watched as the burly sheriff disappeared into the sandstorm as he made his way towards the saloon.

3

The sand swept into the Longhorn as its swing doors rocked on their hinges, yet neither the deadly gunmen nor their surviving captives noticed. The wind howled like a pack of timber wolves all around the large wooden structure as Bart Savage shook the spent casings from his smoking gun before pulling fresh bullets from his belt and sliding them into its hot chambers.

There were four dead people on the floor of the saloon and three times that number still huddled together against the far wall. Savage did not take his eyes from the shaking men as he snapped the gun's cylinder of death back into the frame of the six-shooter.

Griff Reynolds had ridden with Savage longer than any of the others and knew that when the leader of their gang started killing he rarely stopped until he ran out of ammunition.

'How many of these varmints do you figure on killing, Bart?' Reynolds asked. He placed his whiskey bottle down and turned his back on the other outlaws. 'Seems to me like a real waste of bullets.'

Savage twirled the gun on his finger before pushing it down into its holster. He grunted and nodded.

'I like to think of it as target practice, Griff,' Savage replied. He glanced at the rocking swing doors. 'That storm ain't getting no better.'

'You figure that barkeep will go to the Bar 10 and tell Johnny that we're waiting for him, Bart?' Reynolds pushed a cigar into the corner of his mouth and then struck a match with his thumbnail. He raised the match and sucked in smoke.

Savage nodded again. 'I think that bartender will do exactly as I told him. He looked too yellow to disobey me.'

'You ought to slow up your killing, Bart,' Reynolds suggested as a line of smoke trailed from his mouth. 'You'll run out of targets otherwise.'

Savage dragged a chair towards him and sat down upon it.

'There's always some critter to shoot at, Griff.'

Two more of the gang walked to where their undisputed leader sat. Both Sly Potter and Dave Travis were amused by the sight of the four dead bodies spread out on the sawdust.

Savage glanced up at them. 'What you varmints want? I told you to drink your fill. We got us plenty of time to kill.'

'Me and Dave here was wondering if this town had a bank, Bart,' Potter said. 'Seems a real shame to visit a town and not rob its bank.'

Savage narrowed his eyes. 'We'll have us plenty of time to rob the bank, Sly. First we gotta deal with Johnny Mason.'

Travis lifted his bottle to his mouth and swallowed a mouthful of the fiery amber liquor. 'You reckon this Johnny Puma critter is really Johnny Mason, Bart? That old-timer was a real drunk and he might have been just telling you things he figured you wanted to hear.'

'Yeah, that could be right,' Potter agreed. 'Some drunks are real smart at getting folks to buy them whiskey by spinning yarns.'

Savage exhaled. 'He was telling the truth, boys. Johnny Mason is the cowpoke on the Bar 10. When he gets here you'll see for yourselves. Mark my words, we're gonna kill the bastard who gunned down my brothers.'

Reynolds looked down at Savage. 'Don't forget, I lost me a brother as well, Bart. Just like you done.'

Savage looked at his men, then drew his gun faster than any of them could blink an eye. Without taking his eyes from his men Savage cocked and fired his gun at the saloon's remaining patrons. One of them screamed in agony before stumbling forward and falling in a heap on to the four other bodies.

'Get back to your drinking, boys,' Savage commanded.

They did.

4

Hardy Willis could not see a thing as he fought against the gusting wind and blinding sand in his attempt to reach the Longhorn saloon and stop the mindless slaughter. He reached the opposite side of the street and tripped over the boardwalk edge before coming to a halt against the wall of the hardware store. The lawman gripped his deadly shotgun in both hands, leaned against its wall and vainly tried to see the distant saloon. The sand mercilessly whipped the lawman from all sides as he spat at the boardwalk and once again continued his valiant approach. Another gunshot rang out ahead of him.

The sheriff hesitated for a few seconds. He now knew exactly where the shots were coming from. They were indeed emanating from the Longhorn.

Willis steadied himself. Every sinew in his body screamed at him to turn and put as much distance as he could between himself and the place where a dozen vicious killers were slaughtering their captives.

The words of the blacksmith were true.

For a man who seldom ever had to face danger, to confront even one lethal gunman was suicidal. To go up against a whole herd of them was total insanity, yet he had to do it.

Willis refused to dwell on the situation he had found himself in. To do so was to acknowledge the fact that he was closing in on his executioners.

The lawman forced himself forward against the wind.

The closer he got to the saloon the more he realized that every store he had staggered past had been locked and shuttered. The store owners had heard the gunplay just as he had done and were hiding in terror, knowing that soon they too might become a target for the brutal slayers.

The sheriff rested next to a corner.

Through the waves of sand that swept down the street he could see the string of outlaws' horses tethered outside the saloon. He attempted to count them but it was futile.

Just as Joel Harker had implied, there were a lot of them. Maybe a dozen. Maybe more. Willis held the shotgun across his chest and glanced up the gap between the saloon and the wooden building against which he was leaning.

He knew every inch of Sutter's Corner like the back of his hand. Each evening since he had first had the sheriff's tin star pinned to his chest he had walked every street and alleyway. The lawman knew that he could find his way around the town blindfolded if required, and on a day like this one that skill might be the one thing that could save his bacon.

Willis rubbed the sand from his face and began to walk up the narrow alley which, he knew, led to the back of the saloon.

The intrepid lawman was being

knocked nearly off his feet by the buffeting sand but like the man he had always been, Willis would never quit. A feeling that he had not experienced since his younger days overwhelmed him. It had been years since he had actually felt as if he could fulfil his obligation to those who paid his meagre salary. He was the champion of the people of Sutter's Corner.

Willis made his way to where he knew the Longhorn's outhouse stood, at the rear of the building in the alley.

Many men pinned tin stars to their vests but few ever truly put their very lives on the line for those whom they were paid to protect. But Willis had always risked his neck when the need arose.

During all the years he had been sheriff he had never doubted that what he did was worthwhile. The sheriff staggered to the corner of the rear wall of the saloon and inhaled the stench of its outhouse.

He could not see it but knew exactly where it was.

Willis leaned on the weathered wall of the Longhorn and screwed his eyes up until they were barely slits in his sand-beaten features. Every few seconds he managed to see a brief glimpse of the back door of Longhorn.

He spat again and lowered his head. The brim of his well-secured hat flapped as the devilish wind vainly tried to rip it from his head. There was only one way that he knew of to enter a building filled with heavily armed gunmen without getting killed instantly and that was to find an alternative way into it.

A wry smile hid beneath the mask of sand that covered his face as his squinting eyes focused on the rear door, which rocked back and forth on its tormented hinges.

The sheriff knew that it offered him the best chance of not dying too quickly before he achieved his goal. Even so the odds of his living more than a handful of minutes after he ventured into the saloon were mighty slim.

The door rocked even more violently as the sandstorm increased its ferocity. Willis mustered every scrap of his courage. He knew he would be walking into the jaws of death once he entered the Longhorn, but it was his only choice.

His index finger curled around the twin triggers of the shotgun and his thumb pulled the hammers back until they locked into position.

As the sound of the hammers clicking filled his ears Willis walked towards the saloon's rear door. He was committed to whatever fate had in store for him.

Sheriff Hardy Willis was ready.

5

The rear door of the Longhorn moved as though it had a life of its own as it fought against the driving wind that had already ripped most of the screws from its top hinge. Sheriff Willis moved through the blinding sand towards it with his shotgun tucked under his right arm. His finger was curled around the pair of triggers in readiness as he reached the door and gripped it with his free hand.

The lawman could feel the power of the storm as it tested the muscles of his left arm. He stepped inside the saloon like a man walking towards his own gallows. He released his grip on the door, then stepped forward. There was one more door in front of the sheriff. He knew that this door led into the saloon's long main room: the place where Willis knew the outlaw gang was executing innocent victims.

Willis wanted to turn and run away from the inevitable, but he knew that he could not do that most simple of things and yet remain true to the man he believed himself to be. It would be a betrayal of everything he stood for. It would be the act of a coward, and the rotund man had never been afraid of anything. Willis leaned on the door and pressed his ear up against its flaking surface.

Sheriff Willis could hear the raised voices of the men he had come to stop. They were laughing. Even through the door the lawman could smell the acrid aroma of fresh gunsmoke. Another, more sickening scent also filled the flared nostrils of the rotund sheriff.

It was the smell of death.

The lawman inhaled deeply. Sweat ran down from the band of his hat as it clung to his balding hairline. It dripped from his nose on to the barrels of the gun in his hands as Willis attempted to work out how he was going to round up a dozen dangerous killers without ending up dead himself. The truth of the matter was that these were a breed of men who were seldom ever taken alive. They fought to the death rather than face a hangman's rope.

Willis summoned all his resolve but knew that one mistake would be his last. He could hear the raised voices of Savage and his men as they taunted their remaining captives like cats toying with cornered mice.

The lawman's blood began to boil. He could hear grown men sobbing and begging for mercy. Yet Savage and his cohorts had never shown any of their victims mercy. This brutal torture had to stop, he resolved. Whatever the price he would be forced to pay, he was willing to pay it.

The odds were stacked against him and the sheriff realized that blood-chilling fact only too well.

The words of the burly blacksmith filled his mind.

It was suicidal.

Even so it could no longer be shied

away from. Sheriff Hardy Willis lifted his right boot and kicked at the door with every scrap of his strength.

The door and most of its frame shattered into a thousand fragments and fell into the saloon's long room. Willis followed with the deadly shotgun held at hip height. He knew the layout of the long room better than most.

Every inch of its design was branded into his memory.

Defying his age and shape the sheriff threw himself on to the sawdust-littered floor, rolled over what was left of the door and came to a rest next to a card table.

The outlaws had been taken by surprise.

Maybe it was the whiskey that had lulled them into a false sense of security. It might have been the constant sound of the storm, which battered the saloon and sounded like a freight train at full throttle.

Whatever the reason the three outlaws closest to the kneeling lawman had little time to react to his unexpected arrival.

As they each went for their guns Willis pulled on both triggers.

The saloon rocked as both barrels of the mighty weapon blasted their lethal venom at the bar counter where the closest of the outlaws stood. Each of the trio of men was virtually cut in half by the fiery shafts of buckshot.

The long mirror directly behind them shattered as shot and gore were propelled into it. Before the dead men had fallen into the blood-soaked sawdust Willis had swiftly expelled the shotgun's spent shells and rammed two more into the smoking chambers.

With a speed that only a man determined to survive could equal, Willis snapped the shotgun's barrels shut and cocked its hammers again. Then through the swirling clouds of gunsmoke the panting lawman saw the remaining outlaws leap in all directions, seeking cover.

The sheriff turned the card table over

and huddled behind it. Willis knew that it could not protect him from their bullets but it did offer him a place where he could hide unseen for a few moments.

The sheriff's mind raced. He had no plan apart from killing before he himself was killed. So far he had managed to send three of the gang on their journey to the bowels of Hell but there were still a few more of them scattered around the large saloon.

Willis could hear them moving. Their spurs betrayed them but they were all around the long room. Most had found refuge behind the sturdy bar counter, whilst others had turned tables on their rims just as he had done himself.

The sweating lawman had expected a volley of bullets to be fired at him as soon as he had blasted his shotgun at them, yet so far there had been no reply.

Not one six-shooter had been fired back at him since he had killed the three outlaws closest to him. He wondered when their bullets would seek him out.

It was a chilling thought.

Willis tried to swallow but there was no spittle in his tinder-dry mouth.

Fear was choking him and his heart raced but he was alert and poised. It was too late for fear. He had entered the dragon's den and could only pray that his god loved him more than theirs liked them. The more he considered the predicament that he had willingly entered into in an attempt to stop the slaughtering of further innocents, the more Willis began to doubt that these creatures were human at all. Only depraved animals killed the way this gang did. They killed for the sheer sport of it. To them everyone was fair game.

Willis clutched his shotgun and listened to the howling of the wind, which was powerful enough to cause the wooden chandelier in the middle of the ceiling to sway on its chains.

The lawman squinted across to the bar counter. What remained of the shattered mirror allowed the kneeling lawman to see the reflections of the handful of innocent townspeople in its jagged shards.

They were huddled against a far wall, waiting to die like the others. Willis tilted his head. He then saw the pile of dead bodies resting in a pool of their own blood.

Every one of his worst expectations had been proved true. Bob Charles had not been exaggerating when he had spoken to the blacksmith. The monstrous Bart Savage and his cronies had been executing the saloon's customers, just as he had told Harker.

A wave of trepidation overwhelmed the crouching lawman as he pushed the tail of his topcoat over the grip of his holstered six-shooter.

Even the incessant wind, which was blowing clouds of sand into the Longhorn, could not mask the smell of death from the fearful lawman.

'What the hell have I bitten off here?' Willis whispered to himself as he tried to work out where the rest of the gang were. The wind howled like a pack of ravenous timber wolves all around the saloon. It was only mid-afternoon but it was as dark as night outside the Longhorn.

His sand-filled eyes searched the room. The bar counter was horseshoe-shaped, which enabled patrons to wander around it on both sides of the large room. At least half a dozen of the outlaws were somewhere behind the solid wooden counter. Willis was well aware that no amount of buckshot could penetrate the dark-stained joinery and find any of those secreted there. The men who had taken cover behind upturned tables were a different matter, though. Just like himself they had only an inch of wood separating them from a deadly bullet. One well-aimed shot would breach the flimsy barricades.

Willis could hear spurs moving around the far side of the bar counter. He turned and aimed the hefty weapon at the end of the bar, closest to where he knelt.

The first head that poked out from behind the dark-stained mahogany would get blown off its owner's shoulders, he silently vowed.

His finger trembled on the twin triggers of his shotgun in readiness. Beads of sweat rolled down his face as he defied his desire to fire the brutal weapon. Willis waited for what felt like an eternity.

He heard more movement. It did not come from behind the bar counter but from beyond the upturned tables close to the swing doors.

Suddenly in deafening unison a volley of bullets came from the barrels of four of the outlaws' six-shooters. The top of the upturned table rocked as a half-dozen bullets tore chunks out of it above Willis.

He ducked.

Hot splinters showered over his crouching figure as another of the deadly gang emerged from the far side of the bar counter, where Willis was already aiming his shotgun. The sheriff spotted the .45 before he saw the outlaw.

Without a moment's hesitation Willis squeezed one of his shotgun's triggers. A deafening flash of buckshot greeted the outlaw before he had time either to aim or fire his Colt.

The fearsome blast spewed fiery venom at the side of the bar counter. The outlaw was decapitated by the merciless shot. Within a heartbeat Willis had swung around and fired the remaining barrel of his shotgun over the top of the damaged table. The outlaws closest to the swing doors sucked on sawdust as the buckshot tore tables and chairs apart in search of fresh targets.

Using the choking cloud of gun-smoke as cover Willis forced his hefty bulk up and ran across the distance between the table behind which he had sheltered and the horseshoe-shaped bar counter. A handful of shots vainly tried to hit the labouring lawman but all they managed to hit was the far wall. The sound of glass shattering filled the room as picture frames were blown to bits.

Willis dropped down beside what was left of the dead outlaw. He knelt and swiftly jerked the mighty barrels of the shotgun down. Two smoking spent cartridges flew over his shoulder. Willis could feel the blood soaking through the knees of his pants.

Gasping for air the sheriff rammed two fresh shotgun cartridges into his smoking barrels. He had no sooner snapped the weapon together again than another barrage of bullets ripped what was left of the card table apart. The table fell in two parts on to the floorboards.

The wily sheriff suddenly realized that if he had remained there he too would have been torn apart. Sweat soaked his clothing as Willis wondered how long his luck would hold out.

Somehow he was still alive and unscathed. That in itself was a miracle, but in truth Willis had never believed in miracles. He gripped his red-hot shotgun and prayed to a god he had also never believed in until this very moment.

At the far end of the bar counter, sitting on the ground amid the swirling smoke Bart Savage looked at what remained of his gang. There were just seven left intact.

Savage growled like an angry bear. His nostrils flared as he held both his guns in his hands and stared at the sawdust between his legs. Dave Travis moved closer to his leader and reloaded his smoking gun.

'Who the hell is that, Bart?' Travis snarled. He knelt beside Savage's shoulder. 'It sure can't be Johnny Mason?'

'What we gonna do, Bart?' Sly Potter asked his brooding leader. 'Whoever that damn varmint is, he's got us pinned down here.'

'He's also killed four of us,' Reynolds added. 'We're being whittled down real fast.'

Savage darted his gaze at Potter and the others. There was a madness in his eyes that each of those who rode with the deadly outlaw recognized.

Bart Savage was the most dangerous

of creatures at the best of times, but when riled he became a maniac. He would kill anyone when he was cornered. No one was safe, not even those who rode with him.

'We ain't the ones pinned down, boys,' Savage hissed, like a sidewinder ready to strike with venomous fangs. 'That critter just thinks he's got us pinned down. There are still eight of us and only one of him. By my reckoning we got him pinned down.'

The outlaws flanking Savage nodded in agreement.

Savage got slowly to his feet and defiantly looked down across the top of the long, curved bar counter. He had no fear of being shot, as sane men had. In all his days he had never even been wounded, not even in the most brutal of gun-fights. Savage inhaled deeply. He had just one thought in his mind: to kill the man who had somehow managed to reduce his gang by a third in only a few minutes.

'Get on your feet, boys,' Savage

ordered. 'We're gonna kill that bastard.'

The seven remaining outlaws looked at Savage in disbelief as he lowered his chin and continued to glare towards the far end of the long counter.

'Get up on them boots of yours,' Savage snarled. He waved the barrels of his guns at his kneeling men. 'Are you all yella? Are you scared of a man with a scattergun? We've faced worse than that.'

Reynolds cleared his throat and looked up at Savage, who was still openly challenging anyone to try and shoot him. 'So far that man has killed four of our boys with that scattergun, Bart. Even a drunken halfwit can kill with one of them damn things. A man don't even have to aim. Them things just kill when you pull on the triggers. He killed Joe, Bob and Chaz with one shot. He'd have killed more if we'd been closer.'

'Scatterguns kill real bad,' Travis said, and sighed.

'So do I. So do I.' Savage felt his

whiskered chin resting on the knot of his bandanna. 'Now get up on your feet or I'll start killing you all by myself. I want you to split into two groups and rush him from both sides of this bar counter. He can't kill us all.'

Potter gulped. 'He'll sure try.'

'I got me a plan,' Savage said.

'What are you intending on doing, Bart?' Travis asked fearfully as he rose reluctantly to his full height beside the snorting Savage. 'When we rush that bastard on both sides of this counter, what will you be doing?'

Savage looked at his men, who rose to their feet as his waved his weapons in their direction.

'I'm gonna kill him.'

6

The storm was growing more intense. The wise could feel it in their bones. The vast sky was filled with clouds of every hue and they were moving in all directions. Distant thunder echoed across the Bar 10 and it was heading towards the ranch with each beat of the onlookers' hearts. The horsemen who rode across the increasingly windy range towards the ranch house and outbuildings knew that this was a dangerous time of the year, but none of them realized that the true danger lay west of the Bar 10 in the sprawling town of Sutter's Corner. It would eventually make anything the weather had in store for them seem futile.

The ancient Tomahawk straddled his black gelding and led both Johnny Puma and Happy Summers into the very heart of the courtyard. He did not stop spurring until they had ridden into the large barn. The bewhiskered old man dismounted first and shook himself like a hound dog after it has got wet. Sand fell from the wily Tomahawk as his wrinkled eyes watched his younger companions easing themselves from their own horses.

'When do you figure this storm will ease up, Tomahawk?' Happy asked the old man, who was resting a hand on his lethal Indian hatchet. 'We could hardly find enough steers out there to make a bowl of stew.'

'It'll be over before sundown,' Tomahawk answered with a nod of his head. He rested a hand on the tall stable doors and stared at the clouds of sand that kept sweeping across the centre of the ranch.

'You said that yesterday, Tomahawk.' Johnny smiled as he released his cinch straps and dragged his saddle off the back of his pinto. 'And the day before.'

Tomahawk gave a toothless smile. 'And I'll say it tomorrow as well if'n it don't stop blowing.'

Happy rested his own saddle on a stall rail, then moved to Tomahawk's horse and raised its fender. 'If this storm keeps up we'll have to delay the cattle drive, by my reckoning.'

Tomahawk nodded. 'Yep.'

Suddenly all three cowboys heard the door of the ranch house open and turned to look. With the wind still blowing a cloud of sand across the courtyard none of them could see the building, or the tall man who was walking towards them until he emerged from the yellow wall of sand and entered the livery.

Gene Adams rubbed his eyes, looked at the three windswept cowboys and silently nodded. Each of them touched the brim of his hat as the tall rancher walked to a bale of hay and sat down.

'What's wrong, Gene boy?' Tomahawk asked, resting his bony backside down next to his oldest friend. He had known Adams too long not to recognize when the white-haired rancher was troubled. 'You look like you got something gnawing at your innards.'

'Nothing.' Adams smiled. It was forced and did not convince any of the cowboys that it was genuine.

'Don't go handing me that,' Tomahawk pressed. 'Something is troubling you, boy. Spit it out.'

Adams leaned back and looked at Johnny. 'Remember a long time ago when me and Tomahawk first met you, Johnny?'

Johnny gave a slow nod. 'You mean when you and Tomahawk found me all shot up and saved my bacon, Gene? That ain't a time a man can easily forget.'

Tomahawk elbowed Adams. 'We said we'd never talk about that, Gene boy.'

Happy Summers edged towards his three companions.

'What's all this about Johnny being all shot up?' he asked curiously. 'I never heard about that before.'

Tomahawk waved a finger at Happy. 'This ain't none of your business,

Happy. Keep your nose out of this.'

The rancher sighed and placed a hand on Tomahawk's bony shoulders. 'Ease up, Tomahawk. I know that we said we'd never speak on them days, but something has cropped up.'

Johnny moved closer to the two seated men. 'Tomahawk's right, Gene. We always said that we'd not speak about that.'

Gene Adams stood up. He towered over Johnny as their eyes locked. 'I had me a visitor earlier.'

'Who?' Johnny wondered.

'Bob, the bartender from Sutter's Corner was here,' Adams whispered. 'He come riding in here and had himself a real bad story to tell.'

'I didn't even know he could ride a horse,' Tomahawk quipped.

'He can't,' Adams said.

Johnny pushed his hatbrim back. 'And this story concerns me somehow?'

'It sure does, son,' Adams told him. 'Bob said there was a gang of critters in his saloon and they'd already killed two folks, including Maisie the bargirl. They're looking for you and they sent him here to tell you to come to town.'

Johnny looked grim. 'Who are they?'

'You recall a Bart Savage, Johnny?' The rancher could see the memories flood back into the young man's face.

Johnny rubbed his jaw as a hint of tears filled his eyes. 'I sure do. He killed my sweetheart and everyone in Rio Maria apart from me.'

Happy lowered his head and walked away from the three other men. He had heard more than he cared for.

Tomahawk eased his old body off the bale of hay and walked to the youngster's side. His bony fingers rested briefly on the cowboy's arm and he shook his head sadly.

Johnny inhaled deeply and looked up at the rafters. Then he returned his gaze to the troubled ranchers.

'Savage wants me, so I reckon it would be darn impolite to disappoint the bastard, Gene.' The cowboy sighed and rested both hands on the twin grips of his matched pair of holstered .45s. 'I'll saddle a fresh mount and head on to Sutter's Corner before he kills any more innocent folks.'

As Johnny turned he felt the powerful grip of a black-gloved hand on his arm. He stopped and looked hard into Adams's face.

'I gotta go, Gene. You know that. He wants me and he ain't going to stop killing until I show.'

'He ain't alone, Johnny,' Adams hissed. 'He has eleven men with him and this ain't going to be a showdown. Savage intends slaughtering you.'

Johnny shrugged. 'I ain't figuring on committing suicide. I'll take down as many of them varmints as I can before they finish me.'

'You ain't going alone, son,' Adams growled. 'I'm going with you.'

Tomahawk shuffled towards them. 'And you ain't leaving me here to twiddle my thumbs. I'm tagging along.'

Happy turned round. 'Can I come with you boys? I don't know about none of this but I sure don't like men that kill womenfolk.'

A tangle of mixed emotions filled the young cowboy's heart. Johnny Puma inhaled deeply and walked to the barn doors. The sandstorm was still as blinding as ever. He stared at it, then tilted his head and looked over his shoulder at his three friends.

'Why would anyone want to ride with a man who has a dozen gunmen waiting to open up on him with their guns and use him for target practice?' Johnny asked. 'That's plumb loco.'

'Maybe we like you, Johnny,' Gene Adams said.

Tomahawk moved to the side of the tall rancher. He screwed up his wrinkled eyes.

'I'll go see how many hands there are in the bunkhouse, Gene boy.'

Adams gripped his friend's thin arm. 'Don't waste your time, Tomahawk. None of the other hands have returned from out on the ranges. I figure they're all taking shelter in the line shacks until this storm eases up.'

Tomahawk's bearded jaw dropped. 'You mean we is the only ones here to ride with Johnny?'

Adams gave a brisk nod. 'Yep. We'll see if any of our boys are holed up in the line shack between here and Sutter's Corner. If they are we'll get them to tag along.'

'That's a mighty big 'if', Gene boy,' Tomahawk reasoned. 'Them boys could be anywhere in this sandstorm.'

'You fret too much.' Adams tugged on his friend's jutting beard. 'No wonder you got so many wrinkles.'

Tomahawk sniffed. 'Darn tooting.'

Johnny had heard the brief conversation and shook his young head. 'Damn it all. I can't let you boys ride into this trouble.'

The rancher looked at the youngster. A smile traced his face as he raised a gloved finger and pointed at Johnny.

'You can't stop us, son. When anyone picks on any of the riders of the Bar 10 he picks on us all. Whoever Bart Savage is he sure don't know us but he'll learn.'

Tomahawk shook his head thoughtfully. His right hand drew the ancient Indian hatchet from his belt and his eyes studied it. The old man had become an expert with the weapon that had earned him his name. He traced a thumb across its honed edge, then slid it back into its resting place against his skinny hip.

'I knew that one day that boy's history would come looking for him, Gene boy,' he said. 'I just never figured it would be like this, though.'

Adams narrowed his eyes and rubbed his jaw. 'You're right, old-timer. I don't like the thought that innocent folks are being murdered. There ain't no call for that.'

'Why'd this Savage *hombre* wanna kill a female for, Gene?' Tomahawk asked sadly. 'She was such a pretty little thing.'

Adams glanced at Johnny's face. It was drained of all colour and expression. Johnny was totally stunned by the news that Gene had just imparted to him.

'Some folks have a sickness in them, Tomahawk. I reckon this Bart Savage must be the sickest critter the Devil ever spawned.'

Tomahawk slapped his bony hands together.

'We'll feed and water the nags, rub the critters down, then head on to town,' he said.

'There ain't no time for that, Tomahawk,' Adams told him firmly. He turned and looked at the younger cowboys. 'Happy and Johnny can saddle three fresh mounts for you all to ride and I'll saddle my mare.'

'I'll get the horses out of the stalls, Johnny,' Happy told his pal.

Johnny moved across the barn towards Adams. He could not hide the anguish he was feeling at the thought of any of his pals getting hurt, or worse.

'This is my fight, Gene,' Johnny said.

'Savage shouldn't have gunned down innocent folks, son,' Adams argued. 'He made it personal, doing that.'

'This might be costly, Gene. We can't tell how this will pan out. Savage is a mighty bad *hombre* and so are the critters he surrounds himself with. I ain't happy at any of you tangling with them.'

There was a long silence, then Adams rested a hand on the youthful shoulder.

'Just make sure your guns are loaded, son,' the rancher said in a low drawl. 'I got me a feeling we'll need every bullet we got. Now saddle some fresh horses. We got us a score to settle.'

Johnny Puma nodded.

7

The seven outlaws were more fearful of Bart Savage than of the shotgun, which had already claimed the lives of four of their number. The heavily armed men reluctantly moved to the side of their leader and waited. Savage leaned into them as his eyes stared at the remaining hostages huddled together just beyond the pile of dead bodies.

A monstrous idea had just dawned on him. It was one that only a man who valued his own life above all others could ever have conceived. A twisted grin crawled across his scarred features.

'Go grab them snivelling critters and bring them over here,' Savage said in a cold snarl. 'They're gonna be your shields, boys. Whoever that scattergun-toting varmint is at the far end of the bar, I don't think he'll be willing to kill them, but he'll have to if'n he wants to shoot you. Savvy?'

The outlaws all nodded. They strode up to those who were left of the saloon's terrified patrons, grabbed hold of them and brought them back to the bar counter. Savage waved his guns to indicate that his men move to each side of the horseshoe-shaped bar counter with their captives. Then he turned to stare down to where he knew the man with the shotgun was hiding.

'Remember to keep these bums between you and that scattergun, boys,' Savage warned.

Travis had his fingers gripped firmly on to the bandanna of the man he had chosen to use for cover. A man who just happened to be the fattest of the entire bunch.

'This is gonna be real sweet, Bart,' Travis said. 'I sure can't see buckshot getting through this critter.'

Savage nodded in agreement and looked down the length of the long bar.

'Whoever you are, listen up,' Savage yelled out at the top of his voice.

'I'm the sheriff and I'm listening,' Willis shouted back, wondering what would happen next. 'Spit it out, whatever it is you're trying to say. I'd hurry up if I was you 'coz I'm gonna start killing more of your stinking gang darn soon.'

'I don't think you'll want to go shooting that scattergun at us any more, Sheriff,' Savage taunted. He eased himself up on top of the wet surface of the bar counter and stood amid the debris that littered its wet surface. He leaned forward and could just make out the top of the lawman's hat. 'My boys have plucked this saloon's still-living customers off the wall yonder. They're gonna start walking down towards you with them folks in front of them. If you start blasting again with that scattergun you'll be killing townsfolk. Do you cotton on to what I'm telling you?'

Willis exhaled. He knew exactly what Savage was telling him. The outlaws were using as shields the very people he had come to save.

'Do you savvy, Sheriff?' Savage screamed out. 'You'll have to kill the very critters that pay your wages before you can kill any of us again. You'd best quit right now and throw that scatter-gun aside.'

The lawman tried to think. He peeked round the side of the mahogany counter, then pulled back. Savage was telling the truth for once in his rancid existence, Willis thought.

Then he heard the spurs as the outlaws advanced on both sides of the counter. They were on their way to where he knelt.

'You've gone real quiet there, Sheriff,' Savage yelled out again as he walked along the surface of the wet bar counter to where Willis was taking cover. 'How come? Are you kinda befuddled?'

Willis could hear the advancing spurs growing louder as the outlaws drew nearer. Somehow the deranged mind of the outlaw leader had outwitted him. There was no way he could fend them off without killing what was left of the saloon's remaining customers.

Willis shook his head.

'Let them go. You want a hostage? Then take me. Let these innocent folks go,' the sheriff shouted. 'I'm paid to get shot up.'

Bart Savage had moved halfway along the counter top. With each step he could see more and more of his prey from his high vantage point. He trained both his cocked guns at the sheriff's hat.

Savage paused.

'Do you figure that you're a more valuable hostage than all these cowards, Sheriff?' Savage asked. 'Do you? Do you reckon Johnny Mason will value your hide more than these pitiful critters?'

'Who in tarnation is Johnny Mason?' Willis yelled out.

'It don't matter none.' Savage snorted. 'Just show me them hands of yours and I'll let this sorrowful bunch go free.'

The lawman knew that he had no choice but to agree to whatever the crazed outlaw demanded.

'OK. You win.'

Willis raised his shotgun above his head so that all of the outlaws could see it. Reluctantly he tossed the hefty weapon on to the top of the counter.

'I quit. You got the better of me,' Willis called out. 'I can't kill any of the folks who pay my salary. You win.'

'And don't forget to toss away your six-shooter as well, Sheriff.' Savage laughed triumphantly.

Willis drew his handgun and flung it across the saloon. The .45 slid through the sawdust until it hit the far wall.

'I'm unarmed,' the lawman stated reluctantly.

'Good, now stand with them hands held high,' Savage ordered. He watched as Willis slowly stood up with his arms reaching for the tobacco-stained ceiling. The deadly leader of the gang chuckled as he stared down at the helpless lawman.

The sheriff glared up at Savage. 'Now keep your side of the bargain and let these men go.'

The room was suddenly filled with laughter. It was louder than the howling storm outside, which continued to batter the saloon. Bart Savage was more than amused by the innocence of the lawman standing below his high perch. He kicked a pyramid of whiskey glasses over the sheriff. Hardy Willis took a backward step.

'I'm real sorry, but I changed my mind, Sheriff.' Savage walked to the end of the counter. His narrowed eyes studied the rotund lawman. 'I reckon this bunch of worthless dogs might come in useful when Johnny gets here. He might be as pitiful as you and not be willing to shoot them in order to kill us.'

'So you're a liar as well as a madman,' Willis retorted defiantly. 'I figured as much.'

'Which one of us is the locobean? The man with his hands held high or the critter with two cocked guns?' Savage looked angered as he studied the lawman.

'I don't think Johnny will be coming alone,' Willis told him. 'Gene Adams and his Bar 10 riders will be headed here as we speak.'

'Who in tarnation is Gene Adams?' Savage growled.

'You'll find out,' the sheriff replied.

'Hell, you're just a fat old man,' Savage mocked as his men kept firm hold on their prisoners. 'Nothing but a star-packing fat old man.'

Willis nodded and shrugged. 'Yep, I'm just a fat old man who managed to kill four of your gang without even getting winged.'

Each man stared at the other with equal hatred.

'I reckon you've lived as long as most lawmen have a right to,' Savage snarled.

'Maybe even longer.' Willis sighed.

Without warning Savage squeezed on both his triggers, sending two red-hot tapers of lethal lead into the lawman's chest. Hardy Willis buckled and toppled backwards on to the floor next to the headless body of the man he had only moments earlier killed. Soon his blood mingled in the sawdust with that of the fallen outlaw.

'That was good shooting, Bart,' Potter commented.

Bart Savage jumped down next to the stricken Willis and stared at his handiwork. His men dragged their captives closer to where the wounded lawman lay. Their eyes feasted on the sight. The helpless sheriff looked up at Savage with glazed eyes as blood trickled from the corners of his mouth. The devilish outlaw leader cocked his hammers again and spat down upon his victim. A cruel smile stretched across his face as he aimed the smoking barrels at Willis.

'I hate fat old men,' Savage said. 'Especially those who wear tin stars.'

He fired both his guns again. The deafening sound of the two six-shooters unleashing their fury rocked the saloon. The gunsmoke cleared slowly, revealing the sickening sight to the terrified prisoners and their joyous captors.

Willis was dead.

8

Hidden by the cloak of choking sand Bob Charles the bartender reined in beside the tall doors of the livery stable that stood at the far end of the long main street. The sound of the brief gunfight inside the Longhorn saloon echoed in his ears as he dismounted. Charles was still shaking as he led the rented saddle horse into the dark interior of the cavernous building. The sizeable figure of the blacksmith came out from the shadows and the sight of him added to the mounting fear that gripped the bartender.

Charles looked sick as Harker took the reins of the saddle horse from him. Neither man spoke as the horse was led into the depths of the stable. The bartender had delivered the message to Gene Adams, just as Savage had ordered him to do, and had managed to return to Sutter's Corner.

The nervous man sat on the edge of an upturned barrel and buried his face in his hands. He was scared again. The long ride had managed to calm his nerves as he had headed to the Bar 10 but as he had ridden back to the town the horrific reality of what was happening in the normally peaceful town had overwhelmed him.

Charles knew that the rancher would tell Johnny Puma that Bart Savage wanted him. There was no doubt in the mind of the bartender that Adams would not allow the young cowboy to journey to Sutter's Corner alone.

He lifted his face from his sweat-soaked palms and saw the muscular Harker walking back towards him. Charles was panting like a hound. His lungs felt as though they were filled with sand.

'Did you manage to get to the Bar 10, Bob?' the blacksmith asked, pausing beside the bartender.

Charles nodded his reply.

The blacksmith rubbed one of his massive hands on the bartender's head.

'Don't go near the Longhorn, boy,' he advised.

'I didn't figure on going anywhere near the saloon until I see them outlaws leave town, Joel,' Charles admitted. 'I did what they told me to do and I reckon I'm gonna find a real deep hole to hide in until then.'

'That's wise.'

'Did you go and tell the sheriff what's going on, Joel?' Charles asked, managing to rise from the makeshift seat.

A grim expression moulded the features of the burly man as he strode to the tall doors. He stared out into the blinding sandstorm towards the Longhorn.

'Yep, but I sure wish I'd not told Hardy about them ruthless killers.'

Bob Charles wandered to the troubled blacksmith's side and stared at him.

'What you mean?' he asked.

'I told Hardy what you told me,' Harker explained. 'You know him, he got all fired up and grabbed one of his scatterguns and headed to the saloon.'

'But one man couldn't tackle that bunch on his lonesome, Joel,' Charles gasped. 'There are too many of them.'

The larger man nodded. 'I reckon that's why we heard all that shooting a few minutes back. There was one hell of a gun battle in the Longhorn for a few minutes.'

'The shooting has stopped now.'

Harker looked at his friend. 'And Hardy ain't come back out of the saloon. In my book that means only one thing.'

Bob Charles swallowed hard.

'They must have killed him, Joel,' the bartender reasoned correctly. 'They must have done to Willis what they did to little Maisie the bargirl.'

The blacksmith agreed sadly.

'Yep, reckon so.'

Charles clenched his fists in frustrated fury. He felt utterly helpless since he, like so many of the men in Sutter's Corner, was unarmed.

'Damn it all, Joel. If I had me a gun

I'd try and pick some of them critters off. It just ain't right for us to do nothing when them merciless varmints are killing folks with no more fretting than if they were swatting flies in an outhouse. If we only had us some guns.'

The blacksmith knew that the bartender was right. So far the killing had been confined to the Longhorn, but Harker realized that it might soon spread out into the entire town. If it did the streets would be flowing with blood.

'You're right, Bob,' Harker agreed.

'I don't even know anyone in town who owns any weapons,' the bartender added. 'Most of the folks in Sutter's Corner ain't never had any call to arm themselves. Until now, that is.'

Harker looked at the younger man thoughtfully and rubbed his rugged jaw. Then his wrinkled eyes widened. He snapped his fingers.

'I know where there are guns. Plenty of them.'

Charles stepped closer to the mountain of a man. 'Where, Joel? Where are there plenty of guns?'

The blacksmith screwed up his eyes and squinted down the long, barely visible street as sand stung his face like a swarm of crazed hornets.

'Down there in the sheriff's office.' Harker raised an arm and pointed out into the storm. 'That's where.'

The bartender nodded his head.

'Yeah, as I recall there's a wall rack full of rifles in there. The sheriff has repeating rifles and scatterguns as I recall.'

'And there's plenty of ammunition there as well, Bob,' the blacksmith added enthusiastically. 'Are you willing to come with me and rustle up some of them rifles?'

Bob Charles did not have to think of his answer. He nodded.

'I sure am, Joel.'

Both men moved to the rear of the livery stable.

The blacksmith used his strength to force the rear door open against the pounding of the wind. The pair of determined men braved the storm and started to make their way through the alleyways towards their distant goal.

Someone had to try and stop the bloodshed.

The murderous outlaws had to be prevented from adding even more notches to the grips of their weaponry.

Whether the two very different men would be able to stop the Savage gang's murderous progress was something only time and fate knew the answer to.

Soon everyone else would as well.

9

The fertile range resounded with the sound of the hoofs of the galloping horses. The four Bar 10 riders cut a trail through the wall of sand at a pace that only expert horsemen could ever have achieved. The sun was still high in the sky, yet few of its rays seemed to be able to penetrate the dense cloud of sand, which continued to smother the swaying grassland.

The four horsemen had made good time to reach the very edge of the famed cattle spread so quickly, but they knew that with every stride of their valiant mounts they were getting closer and closer to some of the most deadly men any of them would ever encounter.

Every so often there came a lull in the choking storm. It was a brief opportunity for the riders to spit out sand and suck in air. It also allowed them time to try to see the land that stretched out before them and find the small wooden shack they were searching for.

Then as the wind changed Gene Adams caught a brief glimpse of the line shack, a few hundred yards ahead of them. He pointed with his free hand, slapped his reins across the chestnut mare's tail and thundered towards the shack, his three riders in his wake.

The four riders of the Bar 10 eased back on their reins as they approached the small structure, which stood on the fringe of the vast Bar 10 ranch. The line shack had been rocked for hours by the seemingly unrelenting sandstorm. It had lost half its wooden shingles and Gene Adams imagined the remainder would be torn from its sloping roof before the wind eventually eased up.

The rancher handed his reins to Tomahawk and dismounted from the high-shouldered mare. Adams turned his face away from the vicious storm, stepped up on to the porch of the shack and beat on the door.

It creaked opn and Red Evans peered out. He looked startled at the sight not only of Adams but of his three companions.

'What's wrong, Gene?' Evans asked as Chip North moved to stand beside his fellow wrangler.

'I sure hope you ain't sore with us, Gene,' Chip said. 'Me and Red couldn't round up no steers with this damn storm. Every time we got a few longhorns together we lost them in the sandstorm.'

'We figured it was best if we stayed here until the storm ended,' Red added.

'I ain't here for that, boys.' Adams walked into the shack and forced the door shut against the strong wind. He looked at both the young cowboys. 'Johnny needs our help and I was hoping that you boys might want to tag along.'

'I don't understand, Gene.' Chip looked puzzled. 'Why would Johnny need our help?'

Adams looked hard at the two cowboys. 'A gang of outlaws are holed up in the Longhorn saloon over at Sutter's Corner, boys. They want Johnny to go there so they can gun him down. They're killing innocent folks and they'll keep killing until he shows.'

'Why are a bunch of outlaws so all fired up against Johnny?' Red asked.

'Everybody likes Johnny,' Chip said. 'It must be a mistake.'

The rancher frowned. He wiped the caked sand from his features as he contemplated the two loyal cowboys. They deserved to know the truth if he was going to ask them to risk their very lives to help. Adams nodded thoughtfully and moved closer.

'Listen up, boys. What I'm gonna tell you has got to remain between us. A long time ago Johnny had his sweetheart killed by this gang,' Adams revealed. 'He managed to kill a handful of the stinking rats but then got himself shot up. The leader of the gang is a varmint called Bart Savage. He somehow managed to get

Johnny blamed for the atrocities he and his cohorts had done. Johnny became a wanted outlaw.

'Me and Tomahawk found Johnny shot up real bad and nursed him back to health. Since he was wanted I gave him a new name. For the longest while the outlaws thought that Johnny was dead and buried, but somehow they've found out that he's one of my Bar 10 cowboys. They want revenge, boys. They'll do anything to get it.'

'They're killing innocent folks?' Chip gulped.

'Yep.' Gene Adams looked troubled. 'They even killed little Maisie in the Longhorn.'

'I don't cotton to anyone harming females, Gene,' Red said angrily.

'Me neither,' Chip riled.

Adams rested his gloved hands on the shoulders of the two cowboys. 'Me, Tomahawk and Happy wouldn't let young Johnny go there alone. I know this is none of your business but I figured I'd ask if you'd like to ride with us and help him. Will you?'

'How many are there in this gang, Gene?' Red wondered.

'We were told that there are about twelve or more of the critters,' Adams replied.

Red and Chip looked at one another. Neither spoke. Both men nodded, then looked back at the tall rancher.

'I'll tag along, Gene,' Red said. 'Johnny ain't gonna face them killers on his lonesome.'

'Reckon I'll go saddle our horses,' Chip added firmly. 'Somebody has to stop them rats and I'm ready to try. I'd do anything to help Johnny, Gene. Besides, I was mighty fond of Maisie. You can count me in as well.'

Gene Adams smiled warmly.

'Let's go, men.'

★ ★ ★

The thin bartender followed the brawny blacksmith through the maze of back streets until they reached the alley that ran along the side of the sheriff's office. Harker wiped the sand from his face and paused at the corner. The storm was still as fierce as ever and both men were thankful. As long as the air was full of sand they knew that no one would see them as they reached and entered the office.

'Keep close, Bob,' Harker said. He stepped up on to the boardwalk and raced along to the door of Willis's office. His huge hands turned the handle. Both men entered at speed.

The blacksmith closed the door and looked out into the street. It was still impossible to see across to the other side. He glanced at Charles.

'Reckon nobody seen us,' Harker observed.

Bob Charles nodded and rested a hip on the edge of the sheriff's desk.

'Yeah, nobody seen us.'

'We'd be dead if they had,' the blacksmith added. He moved past Charles and looked at the wall rack. There was only one rifle missing from the impressive array of weapons: the one he had seen the sheriff take with him when he had ventured out and headed to the Longhorn.

Charles tilted his head and looked at the rifles. They were just as he remembered seeing them. There were rifles of every kind and all in pristine condition.

'That's one hell of a lot of rifles, Joel.'

Harker pulled some of them off the rack and set them down on the desk. The blacksmith knew little of rifles but he knew enough.

'Are they loaded?' Charles asked.

Harker shrugged. 'I guess so. How do you check?'

The bartender picked up a Winchester. He was quite as naïve about weapons as his companion. He had seen people use rifles but that was as far as his knowledge stretched. He pushed the hand-guard down and squinted into the magazine.

'I reckon this one's loaded.'

Harker leaned over and also peered

into the hole in the side of the repeating rifle.

'You're right, Bob. I can see bullets inside there.'

Bob carefully placed the rifle down next to the others. He watched as the blacksmith plucked a shotgun off the rack.

'Which do you figure is best, Joel? A repeating rifle or a scattergun?' he asked.

Harker sighed. 'Damned if I know. All I can tell you is that Hardy took a scattergun like this one when he went off to the Longhorn. It must be the best or he would have taken a carbine. Right?'

Charles raised his eyebrows.

'The sheriff never came back though, Joel. Maybe he should have taken a Winchester instead.'

The blacksmith pondered for a moment. Then he nodded firmly.

'What if we take one of each?' he suggested.

10

The rear door of the saloon was still battering against its frame as the two outlaws ventured out into the sandstorm and moved like vermin along the rear alley to where they knew they would find the magnificent house that Bart Savage had pointed out to them as they rode into town. Neither had been able to focus too intently upon the mansion on their arrival. Eyes red-raw with blistering, windswept sand could see little, but both of the gang members knew what they were looking for. They were looking for the largest, most ostentatious building on the main thoroughfare.

The Savage gang had only two reasons to be in Sutter's Corner. One was to allow Bart Savage the pleasure of wreaking vengeance on the man who had killed the outlaw leader's three brothers ten years earlier.

The second reason was to rob the town's only bank of every cent within its vaults. Savage had learned years earlier that if you wanted to rob a bank and not run the risk of getting shot you had to adopt a subtle strategy. Instead of entering the bank with guns blazing, you persuaded the banker to bring the money to you.

There was one way in which that could be achieved. You took the one thing bankers prized more than money and then threatened to kill it.

The two outlaws moved through the alley and reached the very edge of the long, wide street. They rested against a high wooden wall and watched as the sand swept along the street in waves.

This was not the first time they had done this. As far as they were concerned it would not be the last. The house was so large that it seemed out of place on the streets of Sutter's Corner. It looked as though it should be set in the middle of a plantation, not situated in an average street.

Both outlaws were about to race across the street when Reynolds grabbed Travis's arm and pointed with his six-shooter to a run-down-looking building. Even with clouds of sand continuing to torment their eyes the deadly gunmen could see the two men with rifles in their hands as they came out of the sheriff's office. The burly blacksmith almost hid the skinny bartender from view as they eased themselves nervously out into the street and looked down towards the saloon.

'See them?' Reynolds hissed. He turned the barrel of his gun in the direction of the pair of rifle-toting men.

'That's the sheriff's office, Griff,' Travis snarled.

'Yep, and they must be his deputies,' Reynolds wrongly assumed. 'I reckon they're figuring on heading down to see what's happened to their boss.'

'I reckon so, Griff.'

Both men moved along the board-walk opposite the office as the two riflemen headed in the direction of the Longhorn. With each step the outlaws took they kept their guns trained on Harker and Charles.

The storm seemed to be reaching its peak. It was howling like demented banshees. The sand was swirling around like twisters. Yet neither Reynolds nor his comrade allowed it to slow their pace.

Harker and Charles were nervously approaching the saloon whilst both the outlaws were moving at speed. In a few moments the two pairs of men were directly across the main street from each other.

'Hey!' Reynolds yelled out at the top of his voice, struggling to be heard against the deafening roar of the storm.

Harker heard the voice and turned his bulky frame. Charles caught a brief glimpse of the two men standing outside the shuttered barber shop.

'Who are they?' the bartender asked.

It was the last question he would ever ask.

Like rods of lightning a series of bright flashes carved through the sandstorm and hit both Charles and Harker. The larger man shook as his huge body absorbed the flurry of bullets that hit him. The smaller bartender was unable to stand his ground.

One bullet punched him backwards, then a few more knocked him completely off his feet. The sound of breaking glass filled the ears of the blacksmith. Harker fell against a porch upright and clung to it. His dying eyes saw Charles crashing through the windowpanes of a drapery store.

'Bob?' Harker gasped, as if his dead friend might be able to explain what was happening.

Another salvo of lethally accurate bullets tore into the large man. Joel Harker released his grip on the upright. He raised the Winchester in his blood-covered hands and took a faltering step.

Then, like a felled tree, Harker toppled from the porch and hit the ground hard. He lay face down staring helplessly at the two men who had used him for target practice. Between the waves of sand rolling down the main thoroughfare his eyes could see them walking away.

The blacksmith coughed.

Then Harker was dead.

Both Reynolds and Travis had known that there was no point in checking whether the two men they had just filled with lethal lead were still alive.

After a lifetime of killing they instinctively knew when they had achieved their goal.

As though nothing had happened the two outlaws returned to the high wooden wall, which still swayed against the constant onslaught of the storm.

They took shelter behind it and shook the spent casings from their smoking weaponry as they concentrated on the large house once again.

'How come bankers always gotta have themselves the biggest houses, Griff?' Travis asked his companion as they rested against the wall and reloaded their guns. 'That place yonder looks like a castle and no mistake. How many damn rooms do you figure that place has got?'

'Too many.' Reynolds spat as he holstered one gun and pushed fresh bullets into his other .45.

'Now if that was a whorehouse I could see the sense in having a real lot of rooms.' Travis winked.

Reynolds snapped the chamber of his gun shut and spun the still-hot weapon on his finger thoughtfully.

'Reckon most bankers are just plumb boastful, Dave.'

'Seems that way,' Travis agreed. He drew one of his own weapons and cocked its hammer. 'I got me a feeling that the banker won't be needing a house of any size after Bart's through with him.'

Reynolds grinned. 'I'll bet you a hundred bucks Bart kills the banker.'

'I ain't taking that kinda bet, Griff.' Travis pulled his gun hammer back. 'Bart always kills bankers.'

'Come on. Let's go and do what Bart told us to do and catch us some bait.' Reynolds moved away from the wall.

With their guns held firmly in their hands, Reynolds and Travis ran through the cloud of sand that filled the main street of the town towards the big house. Every store had been shuttered and locked soon after the gang's arrival but that meant nothing to either of the outlaws. They had been given their instructions and were following them to the letter.

Both men looked at the finest of all the houses in the town, with a brass nameplate secured to its white picket fence. Travis gave it a side-glance, then nodded to Reynolds.

'This is it, Griff,' he said.

'Yep, this is where the stinking rich old banker lives, OK,' Reynolds agreed. He tore the gate off its hinges and threw it aside. The gusting wind lifted the gate up into the air. It vanished in the dense cloud of swirling sand. 'Let's go visiting.'

Both outlaws fought against the powerful wind and made their way up to the porch. They sheltered in the porch and glared at the large door. Its black surface was so highly varnished that it was like a mirror.

'Reckon the banker won't be living here after we're finished, Dave,' Reynolds gloated.

'That'll teach him to go flaunting his wealth.' Travis grinned. 'It don't pay to look down on poor folks.'

'Quit gabbing and kick this door down,' Reynolds growled. 'I'm sick of chewing on sand.'

'Hold your horses.' Travis clenched a fist and started to pound upon the door. After four mighty raps they heard the lock being released. The door moved ajar and the face of a maid stared through the gap at the two outlaws.

'What you want here?' the woman asked. Then her eyes widened as she saw the barrels of the guns aimed at her.

'Out of our way, woman.' Reynolds pushed the door and they entered. Travis closed the door and spat out sand as he looked around the hall. It was far larger and fancier than any that they had entered before. 'Your master must be a better thief than we are to afford a shack like this.'

'The master is at the bank,' the maid stammered.

'We know that,' Reynolds said. 'It ain't him we come to see, woman.'

The shaking maid lifted her long apron and held it to her face as if its thin fabric might protect her from whatever it was the two outlaws intended doing.

'Don't hurt me. I ain't got nothing,' she said.

Reynolds grunted. 'We don't want you either.'

'Where's your mistress, you stupid woman?' Travis asked. He pushed the barrel of his gun between her ample breasts. 'Tell us where she is or I'll blow a hole in your chest big enough to ride a horse through.'

Her large eyes flashed from one of the deadly outlaws to the other.

'What you want with Mrs White?' the terrified maid asked nervously.

Griff Reynolds angrily grabbed hold of the woman and smashed her against a wall. He placed the barrel of his gun against her temple and glared into her eyes.

'Quit stalling, woman. Where is she?' He repeated the question. 'Where's your damn mistress? This is a mighty big house and I don't hanker after searching the whole damn place looking for her.'

The maid's eyes looked towards a closed white door with brass fixtures.

'She's in the parlour, having refreshments,' the maid stammered in a low whisper. 'You ain't gonna kill her, are you? She's a real fine lady and don't deserve killing. Please don't kill her.'

'I got me a feeling she wouldn't beg for your life, woman.' Reynolds stepped back from the maid and looked at the door.

He then looked at Travis. He did not have to say a word for his partner to know what to do. Dave Travis strode to the door and opened it. The perfumed air stopped the deadly outlaw in his tracks. Travis then saw a woman sitting on a well-upholstered double seat behind a small table. A large pitcher of lemonade and a solitary glass rested upon a silvery tray.

A bewildered Martha White stared up at the dust-caked outlaw. Her well-powdered jaw dropped. She was speechless.

Travis looked back at Reynolds. 'I found her.'

Griff Reynolds strode into the parlour and up to the stunned, seated Mrs White. In one swift action he grabbed the banker's wife's arm and hauled her to her feet.

'You're coming with us, woman,' Reynolds snarled. He led the woman into the hall towards Travis, who had already opened the front door.

'What's the meaning of this?' Martha

White eventually managed to ask as she was dragged towards the open doorway. 'Where are you taking me?'

'We're taking you to the saloon,' Travis growled.

The banker's wife screamed in horror as Travis took hold of her other arm.

'Sheriff! Sheriff!'

Both outlaws paused in the doorframe, holding the banker's wife firmly between them. Travis grabbed her face and squeezed her cheeks together until she stopped screaming. He pushed his own snarling face down into hers and hissed like a rattlesnake about to sink its fangs into its prey.

'Don't go wasting your breath, gal. We already killed the sheriff,' Travis told her in a menacing whisper. 'We would kill you just for the fun of it. Now hush up unless you want to make your husband a widower.'

Somehow Martha White knew the words she had just heard were the absolute truth.

Reynolds swung round and aimed his

six-shooter at the maid, who was still pressed up against the hall wall. A cruel smile was carved into his hardened features.

'Listen up, gal,' Reynolds shouted at the maid. 'Are you listening?'

She stared with unblinking eyes at the man who was aiming his gun at her, and managed to nod.

'I'm listening.' She trembled.

'Good. I want you to go to the bank and tell her husband to fill a heap of canvas bags with all the paper money in the bank's vault. No gold coin. Just paper money. Savvy?'

She nodded again and repeated: 'Just paper money. No gold coin.'

Reynolds added: 'Then tell him that he has to bring it to the saloon and we'll let him have his wife back unharmed. If he don't show in thirty minutes we'll kill her and visit the bank with guns blazing anyway. Savvy?'

The maid gave another nod of her head.

'I'll tell him, mister.'

Confident that the chilling message would find the ears of the bank manager, Reynolds and Travis dragged the banker's wife out into the sandstorm.

The maid walked to the open door and looked out nervously into the storm. She watched silently as the two outlaws disappeared into the murk with her mistress in tow.

Her heart pounded inside her large bosom as if it were about to explode. She lifted her shawl off the hatstand and wrapped it around her shoulders.

She ventured out from the handsome house and made her way along the windswept street towards the bank. The outlaws' grim message was branded into her numbed mind.

11

The six riders of the Bar 10 were now close to Sutter's Corner and getting nearer with each long stride of their mounts' long legs. Each of them knew that they would already have reached the sprawling settlement were it not for the blinding sandstorm, which hampered their progress.

Johnny had moved alongside the rancher, ahead of his four fellow cowboys. Their horses were biting at their bits as the fearless horsemen urged them on to a pace that would guarantee their reaching town long before sundown.

There were still a few miles to go.

Plenty of time to think.

Johnny tried to rid his mind of the memories which had haunted him for nearly ten years. It was impossible. The more he tried to dismiss the memories, the more they haunted him.

Gene Adams had given him a new name and a new life, but now, as he rode beside the legendary rancher, Johnny recalled memories of events that he had managed to suppress for over a third of his life.

Johnny had been a skilled marksman since childhood. He had managed to earn his living by hunting and had made enough money to buy himself a pinto pony and a fancy shooting rig before he had reached his fifteenth birthday. For the next few years he had roamed from one place to another, doing odd jobs. Before long the life of the aimless drifter had become ingrained into him.

Yet when he had ridden into the small town of Rio Maria, close to the Mexican border, he had never fired a shot in anger.

There had been no notches on his wooden gun grips. He had only killed animals for their pelts or to put food in his young belly.

Unlike many other drifters Johnny

had always refused to use his intrepid gun skills on his fellow men.

Rio Maria had been a quiet, gentle town of no more than 200 souls when the young Johnny Mason had ridden past its unmarked boundaries.

For some unknown reason Johnny had taken a liking to the town and the people who lived there. He had been a drifter who had survived alone since losing his entire family to the fever. He had set out on a path that had taken him hundreds of miles in search of something he did not even know he was looking for.

He found that certain something in Rio Maria.

Her name was June Lopez. It was not until he had set eyes upon the raven-haired beauty that suddenly the desire to continue roaming evaporated from every fibre of his being.

June was the youngest daughter of the town's sheriff. Before setting eyes upon her Johnny had thought he would continue to travel aimlessly until he had grown too old to do so.

June Lopez had other ideas when she allowed the young Johnny to chase her until she eventually caught him. Love was something neither of the young pair had ever had any experience of, but when they had set eyes upon one another, they knew what it truly meant.

They had been like two sides of the same coin.

Without realizing what was happening to him Johnny stayed his roving and got a job in the town so that he could stay close to her. She had roped his heart and hauled him in without even knowing that she had done so. They were innocents who lived for one another.

For months the pair grew closer and closer until they were virtually inseparable. It was obvious to everyone that the youngsters were destined to marry.

Johnny had never imagined in his wildest dreams that he of all people would willingly settle down anywhere. It was something other folks did: the lucky ones who somehow managed to find their one true love.

Weeks had become months before Johnny realized that he had been in Rio Maria for over a year. His magnificent pair of matched Colt .45s had gathered dust in their holsters while his hand-tooled gunbelt hung from a peg on the wall of the sheriff's office.

June's father had taken a shine to the young drifter and when he saw that his last unmarried daughter was besotted with Johnny, Jose Lopez had taken him on as a deputy.

Like many of the border towns Rio Maria had once been in Mexico, and only existed now because it had been blessed with a ceaseless supply of gold ore and dust. Men still mined the precious metal and fashioned beautiful artefacts from it. Gold had become something none of the inhabitants of the remote town valued as others in the outside world tended to do.

The people of Rio Maria had so much gold at their disposal that they regarded it as just another of the Lord's gifts and no more valuable than any other abundant commodity. It was no different to them than the sweet grass their livestock grew fat upon or the crystal-clear water that flowed in their rivers.

Rio Maria had become a tranquil paradise over the years, whilst most other towns in the ever growing Wild West had taken a more ruthless course.

That tranquillity soon ended when news of the remote settlement's abundance of golden treasures had reached the ears of those who would do anything to get their hands upon the town's precious golden objects.

There were many men with black hearts on either side of the long border who lived by killing and stealing. Creatures without souls whose greed knew no limits to their depths of depravity.

As he drove his mount on towards Sutter's Corner surrounded by his fellow Bar 10 riders, Johnny recalled the day when, out of the shimmering heat haze, the eighteen outlaws had suddenly arrived in the peaceful Rio Maria.

A chill traced his spine.

No matter how hard Johnny tried to shake the sickening memories from his mind they became ever clearer. They tormented him as his mount increased its pace beneath him.

The beautiful memory of June's innocent face was replaced by the horrific recollection of what she had looked like after Bart Savage and his bloodthirsty gang had finished with her.

The young horseman screwed up his eyes and gritted his teeth as the sand whipped his handsome features. Tears trailed from his eyes as Johnny rode on and on. Yet it was not only the blinding sandstorm that tortured him.

Johnny had encountered many men with dark souls before he had drifted into the town of Rio Maria but none of them had been as bad as Savage and his henchmen.

A decade ago Johnny had been forced to use his guns in anger after the merciless Savage gang had destroyed nearly every one of the small town's inhabitants.

Until that moment Johnny had never imagined that he could feel such hatred as he had felt on that day when his beloved sweetheart had been murdered.

Johnny spurred on as his fellow Bar 10 cowboys flanked him and every single one of those horrific visions kept pace with his galloping horse.

The town had been littered with bodies. The streets had turned crimson as they flowed with the blood of those whom Savage and his gang had mercilessly destroyed in their hunt for every scrap of gold in Rio Maria.

All of the townsfolk had been killed so that the outlaws could get their hands on the golden ornaments and jewellery in their small homes.

Like so many other outlaws, Savage had realized that a perfect crime was one where there were no witnesses to point an accusing finger. Johnny had been on an errand for the sheriff that day, and had heard the distant gunfire as he returned to Rio Maria.

That was the only reason he had not suffered the same fate as the rest of the town. He had lost his mind when he had discovered the body of his sweetheart. Grief had turned into a desire for blind vengeance.

Even ten years later it was still as vivid as the fateful day when he had clutched June's limp, blood-soaked body in his arms and nursed her until he realized that his prayers would go unanswered.

The shooting had still been echoing in the tiny town as night had fallen. Johnny recalled how on that day he had lost his senses and strapped on his guns.

Whatever had happened after that was still a blur. He knew that he had somehow survived the encounter with the large gang of vicious killers and had managed to kill some of them before they sent a telegraph message to the Texas Rangers.

Johnny had been blamed for the massacre and within hours was himself a hunted man with a price on his head.

Savage had turned the deputy into a wanted outlaw with one simple message. Johnny had been hunted like a dog and shot to ribbons as he fled from the posse.

He had no memories of what had happened after that until the day when he had awoken in the ranch house of the Bar 10, weeks later. Tomahawk and Gene Adams had cut the bullets from his body and sewn his wounds up. When Johnny told Adams his story the rancher had believed him.

From that day on Johnny had a new name and none of them had spoken of those horrors ever again until the rancher had informed his young friend that Bart Savage had at last tracked him down.

Johnny continued to spur his horse on through the sandstorm next to the men who had become like a family to him over the years. None of the other Bar 10 riders could have ever imagined the horrors that Johnny had vainly tried to forget.

Not even Tomahawk or Gene Adams, who had found him close to death after he had been riddled with the bullets of a posse of misguided lawmen, had an idea of what his young eyes had witnessed or the pain which still dogged his heart.

The six horsemen drew rein on the tree-covered rise and looked down through the gusting storm at Sutter's Corner below.

Adams rubbed the sand from the eyes of his mare and looked at the face of his young pal.

'You ready, son?' he asked.

Johnny nodded. 'I'm ready, Gene.'

The rancher glanced across at the other four horsemen.

'Are you ready?'

There were sounds of affirmation from the cowboys.

Adams touched the brim of his black hat. 'C'mon, you bunch of galoots. We got us some killing to stop.'

Then through the raging wind the keen eyes of Red Evans spied something winding its way along the trail due south of their resting place.

'Lookee yonder, Gene,' Red spluttered, sand filling his mouth. 'Ain't that a stagecoach?'

Adams raised himself in his stirrups and shielded his eyes from the incessant wind. He screwed up his eyes, then gave a nod of his head.

'It sure is, Red. And it's making for Sutter's Corner.'

'We can't let that stage head into town, Gene boy,' Tomahawk piped up. 'The passengers and crew will be massacred.'

Johnny reached across and tugged on Adams's sleeve.

'Tomahawk's right, Gene. I'll stop it.'

The rest of the riders watched as Johnny spurred his mount and thundered down the ridge to intercept the stagecoach before it reached the town.

The rancher swung his chestnut mare round. He looked at his cowboys, then pointed frantically after Johnny.

'Well, what we waiting for? We gotta help that young hothead. C'mon, boys.'

Like valiant knights from a bygone time, the riders of the Bar 10 thundered down towards the ridge in pursuit of Johnny as the determined horseman tried to stop the stagecoach before it reached Sutter's Corner.

12

Johnny Puma rode into the sandstorm atop the high-shouldered saddle horse with no sense of the danger that faced him. He had just one thought in his young mind: to stop the stagecoach before its two-man crew made the mistake of entering Sutter's Corner.

Racing a short distance behind the tail of the powerful mount, the other five Bar 10 riders were closing the distance between themselves and the stagecoach with the same thought in their minds.

They had to prevent the stagecoach being driven into the streets of the town whilst the Savage gang were holed up there.

Failing to stop the long vehicle would be tantamount to signing the passengers' and crews' death sentences. Johnny rose in his stirrups and felt the sharp sand cutting his face. He could barely see the six-horse team through the dense wall of sand but he forged on regardless.

Johnny had not given any consideration to the fact that the vehicle's shotgun guard might assume that any rider who approached the stagecoach at speed might be an outlaw and fair game to shoot at.

The large horse pounded and flattened the tall grass as it galloped towards the long vehicle ahead of it. Unlike Johnny's pinto pony the far bigger horse did not respond as Johnny had hoped it would.

It was skittish and unwilling to blindly obey its new master as his black-and-white pony had always done.

Johnny could sense the fear in the huge horse. He whipped his reins across its tail and tried to encourage the animal to keep travelling at pace.

There was only one thing in Johnny's favour and that was the lie of the trail road that the stagecoach was forced to travel along through the eerie sandstorm.

The road had always seemed to those who travelled along its length as if it had been created by a drunkard. The well-used dirt trail meandered around countless trees as it led to the sprawling town, but for the first time in its history the crooked trail was actually serving a purpose.

It was slowing the stagecoach and aiding the cowboys who were riding at breakneck pace directly towards the vehicle as the driver was forced to steer his vehicle around one bend after another as well as doing battle with the violent sandstorm.

Johnny balanced in his stirrups as his half-closed eyes watched the vehicle's six-horse team negotiate a particularly severe bend in the trail. He dropped down on to his saddle and thrust his spurs into the horse's flesh. The animal leapt over a great fallen tree and on to the dirt trail just ahead of the approaching stage.

The cowboy dragged his reins back as the stagecoach cut a path through the choking dust straight at him and his startled mount. Johnny blinked hard and stared at the snorting lead horses of the team.

It was obvious to the cowboy that neither they nor the driver could see him and his horse.

Desperately Johnny was forced to use every ounce of his strength to make his mount back up even further as the stagecoach's team passed within inches of him.

The wheels of the stage sounded like a buzz-saw as they rolled past the skittish horse. Johnny hung on to his reins as his mount reared up and the body of the coach narrowly missed them. A vortex of dust enveloped the cowboy as he steadied the unfamiliar animal. Johnny angrily dragged his reins hard to his right and slapped the horse's ears.

'Damn it all!' the young cowboy cursed. 'My pinto wouldn't have shied like that. You chickened out there, horse. Come on, you worthless gluepot.'

Johnny spurred.

The horse thundered after the coach. Johnny used his long leathers to whip the animal's shoulders until it was back at full pace.

Through the dust which was being kicked up from the metal wheel rims Johnny saw the canvas-covered tailgate as he started to gain on the swaying stage.

Then to his right he caught a brief glimpse of his fellow Bar 10 cowboys through the clouds of sand as they galloped towards the lead horses of the stagecoach. Johnny drove his spurs into his mount again and, just as the horse drew level with the rear of the stagecoach, he pulled his left boot out of its stirrup and leapt like the wild cat he had been named after.

His gloved hands caught the leather straps that hung down across the luggage rack on the tailgate. For a few moments Johnny just hung on beside the large rear wheel. He then mustered his strength and hauled himself up on top of the canvas and scrambled to the roof of the fast-moving stage.

Gene Adams led his cowboys from the tall grass, then drove his mare up on to the road and reined in. He narrowed his eyes and watched keenly as the six-horse team emerged from the sandstorm.

The rancher held on to his reins firmly and stared at the two men sitting up on the high stagecoach seat. He drew one of his guns and fired a shot heavenward. The deafening crack and bright flash alerted the driver to the rancher's presence.

The driver frantically pushed his boot down on to the brake pole and pulled back on his long leathers.

There was a screeching sound as the brakes of the coach stopped the big rear wheels from rotating. The lead horses were wide-eyed and snorting as they came to a standstill less than spitting distance from the rancher.

'Are you a madman?' the driver yelled out from his lofty perch. 'I could have ploughed right through you.'

'You didn't,' Adams said in a low, confident drawl as he holstered his .45.

Then Adams saw the guard quickly haul his double-barrelled shotgun out from the box at his feet and train the hefty weapon down at him. The rancher still did not show any emotion as he glared at the guard.

'Raise them hands,' the guard ordered. 'Or I'll part your hair right down to your damn belt buckle.'

Before Adams could respond the remaining four Bar 10 riders rode out of the sandstorm and drew rein beside the rancher.

Seeing the shotgun aimed at Adams, Tomahawk dragged his ancient Indian hatchet from his belt and threw the deadly axe at the shotgun guard. The tomahawk flashed through the sand-filled air and knocked the heavy weapon out of the startled guard's hands.

Adams looked at his old pal and slowly dismounted as Johnny stood up on the roof of the stagecoach behind the pair of seated men.

'You were lucky he didn't part *your* hair down to your belt buckle, mister,' Johnny said. He jumped down to the ground, grabbed the reins of his horse and threw himself back on to his saddle. He looked at the nervous guard and smiled. 'Tomahawk's plumb dangerous with that old hatchet of his.'

'Who are you?' the driver called down to the rancher.

'My name's Adams,' the rancher replied. He walked to stand just below the two men. He rested a boot on the small wheel and looked at both men in turn. 'Gene Adams.'

'Of the Bar 10?' the driver asked.

'Yep.' Adams nodded.

'What do you want with us?' the guard asked. He watched Johnny lean from his saddle and pluck the tomahawk up off the sand in one easy action.

Adams rubbed his jaw thoughtfully. An idea had just come to him and he knew it was the best bet he and his men had of getting the better of the Savage gang.

'We want this stagecoach, *amigo*,' the rancher answered.

'Is this some kinda hold-up?' the driver enquired.

'Nope,' Adams replied. 'It ain't a hold-up.'

'Then what do you want the stage for?' The guard piped up nervously. 'We ain't even got a strongbox.'

Tomahawk blinked hard and looked at Adams. 'Why do we want the stagecoach for, Gene boy?'

Adams spat sand.

'Listen up. We just want to borrow the stage for a while. You can have it back when we're finished.'

Johnny steered his mount close to the old cow-puncher and handed the Indian axe to Tomahawk. Tomahawk accepted the return of his hatchet from Johnny as he and the others listened to the rancher.

'There's mighty big trouble in town and by my figuring you'll end up dead if you drive this stagecoach into Sutter's Corner right now,' Adams explained, looking steadily at the faces of the two men on the driver's board. 'There's a gang of the meanest outlaws there and they're killing folks for the sheer fun of it.'

Johnny rode up to Adams, stopped his mount and looked at the rancher. He was as confused as the pair of stagecoach men and the other cowboys. He leaned over his saddle horn and stared at Adams.

'What in tarnation do you want the stage for, Gene?' Johnny asked. 'I thought we were just stopping it from heading into town; just warning them.'

There was a long silence as the rancher pulled up the collar of his topcoat against the wind. He then looked back at Johnny.

'I've got me a plan, son,' Adams explained. 'It means we gotta use this stagecoach.'

'I don't like the sound of that,' Happy piped up.

Chip and Red steadied their mounts. Neither spoke as they watched Johnny lean closer to the rancher.

'Hold on there. Do you intend driving this stage into town, Gene?' Johnny gulped and pointed at the driver and the guard. 'Savage will kill you just the same as he'd kill these two boys. They'll use this stagecoach for target practice as soon as they see it. Tell me you ain't thinking of driving this stage into Sutter's Corner, Gene. That's suicide.'

The head of the Bar 10 nodded as though agreeing with every word that spilled from the young cowboy's lips.

'That's right, but I ain't driving it, Johnny,' Adams said. He turned his attention to Tomahawk. 'He is.'

Johnny Puma straightened up on his saddle and looked at the stunned face of the old-timer.

'What? You're gonna make Tomahawk drive this stagecoach right into the sights of the Savage gang?' Johnny gasped.

'That's the plan,' Adams replied.

Tomahawk opened his toothless mouth. 'Me?'

Gene Adams nodded.

'Yep. You're driving this stagecoach right down the middle of the main street, past the Longhorn, old-timer,' he confirmed.

'That sounds mighty dangerous, Gene,' Red said.

Adams glanced briefly at the cowboy. 'It is, Red.'

Tomahawk scratched his jutting beard and shook his head in disbelief.

'That's gotta be the worst damn plan I've ever heard, Gene boy,' the old-timer grumbled. 'Why me?'

Gene Adams lowered his head, stared at his ancient pal and shrugged.

'Why? Because you're the smallest, Tomahawk. That's why. It's as simple as that.'

The bewildered Tomahawk raised his bushy eyebrows and waved a bony finger at the rancher.

'If I'm still alive after all this you owe me a full glass of whiskey, boy.' He snorted. 'You hear me?'

The rancher looked at the old man.

'Hell, if you're still alive after this I'll

buy you a whole bottle of whiskey, Tomahawk,' Adams drawled. 'Maybe even two bottles,' he added.

'You're gonna buy me two bottles of whiskey?'

'If you don't get yourself killed I am, Tomahawk.' Adams exhaled.

Tomahawk watched as the stagecoach driver and guard clambered down from their high perch.

'You ain't scared are you, Tomahawk?' the rancher asked his old friend.

'I ain't never been scared in my whole life, Gene boy.'

'That long, huh?'

The wily old man frowned and looked at the other Bar 10 riders.

'I still reckon this is a real stupid plan,' Tomahawk whispered to them before dismounting and moving to the stagecoach.

They watched as the bony old man reluctantly climbed up to the driver's seat. Adams turned to the rest of his cowboys and lowered his head.

'Now listen up. For my plan to work

you have to do exactly as I tell you. We're riding into the jaws of death and we can't afford to make one mistake,' Adams told them. 'We're all in the hands of each other.'

The five Bar 10 cowboys listened intently. They knew their very lives depended on one another following the rancher's orders to the letter.

13

The storm began to ease but, like a wild mustang, it refused to quit its bucking altogether. Every few heartbeats a wave of sand lashed out at the buildings and at those who had yet to seek shelter within them. The outlaws' horses, which were still tethered to the hitching rails outside the Longhorn, were in a sorrowful state. Not one of the surviving members of the Savage gang cared one bit about his horseflesh. They knew there were plenty more that they could steal up in the livery stable at the end of the long main street.

For the first time for hours the sun could actually be seen by those who cared to look heavenward. Its rays were at last able to reach the ground. But not one person in Sutter's Corner had noticed.

The town was filled with a fear that was contagious.

At any moment those who hid from view inside the wooden buildings knew that they too could be preyed upon by the gang of deadly killers. The shooting had resounded around the town for hours and every one of the townsfolk knew that the deadly gang of merciless killers could strike out at any of them without fear of retribution.

Many eyes had espied the resolute lawman's battle against the ferocious storm on his way towards the Longhorn. None of those eyes had seen Hardy Willis return but the people had heard the gunfight that had taken place inside the saloon after he had entered it, his shotgun held across his chest.

The sheriff had never been a man to linger anywhere for too long and the simple fact that nobody had seen the rotund lawman return to his office told its own terrifying tale.

Willis had to be dead. There was no other conclusion that could be made. And if the sheriff could not defeat the unholy gang, no one could.

The prospect of any rational person venturing out into the street with an untold number of outlaws still ready and able to kill them deterred any of Sutter's Corner's citizens from succumbing to their curiosity.

Only one man in the town was intent on stepping out into the street and heading to where everyone knew Savage and his gang were holed up.

That man was Joshua White, the bank manager. His hooded eyes glanced through the glass windows of the bank out into the street. The storm was ebbing but the danger for him and his beloved wife was probably increasing with every passing second.

White knew that his life was about to be ripped apart but his obeying the outlaws' demand to deliver all of the bank's money would mean that the lives of everyone who had entrusted him with their savings would also be destroyed.

He watched as his two tellers emptied the last of the vault's paper money from trays into the canvas bags. The banker started to secure the leather straps of each of the six bags as his mind failed to think of a way out of his predicament that would not result in his wife being executed.

Only minutes earlier White had received the message from his distraught servant. He had not wasted one second before ordering his tellers to do just as he had been instructed.

Against every one of his banker's instincts White obeyed the outlaws' demands without question. Between them he and his tellers had filled half a dozen canvas bags with all of the bank's paper money from his vault. White wondered if handing over the bank's entire stock would actually buy his wife's freedom.

If the memory of all of the shots he had heard since the fateful arrival of the Savage gang told him anything it was that there was no amount of cash that could stop killers from killing.

Yet he had to try.

A loyal and faithful husband had to

try, even if the odds were stacked against him.

White stared at the bulging canvas bags. He had secured every buckle of every strap. Every cent of the combined wealth of Sutter's Corner's inhabitants was in the half-dozen bags. Only a few thousand dollars in gold coin remained on the vault's shelves. The banker realized that the outlaws had not wanted the coins because of their being appreciably heavier than the banknotes.

He knew that by handing over the banknotes he was ruining not only his career and his reputation; he was also destroying the lives of every one of the bank's customers.

Only those who kept their money stashed in their homes would be unaffected by his actions.

His eyes darted to the wall clock.

It had taken barely twenty minutes to fill the bags. White stared at the faces of the two tellers and could see that they knew he was a broken man.

They also knew that he could never

carry all of the bags to the Longhorn on his own. The younger of the two tellers stepped towards White.

'Can I help you with these bags, sir?' Ted Smith asked his employer.

Joshua White glanced at the teller. He wanted to refuse the offer but knew he needed all the help he could get in order to achieve his goal.

'I'm much obliged, Ted,' White said.

'Reckon I'd best give you a hand as well,' Ty Logan, the other teller, said with a nod. 'Two bags apiece is just about manageable, I guess.'

The banker was touched by the loyalty of his employees. He was also fearful of the risk to their safety if they assisted him. He gave a nod of his head.

'Thank you, men. I can't tell you how much this means to me.' He sighed. 'But when we unload these bags at the saloon I want you to run for your lives. Promise me that.'

'Don't worry, sir,' Ted Smith assured him as he unlocked and opened the door. 'We'll run as fast as we can.'

'I sure hope they let Mrs White go, sir,' Logan added.

'You and me both, Ty,' White stammered.

The sandstorm was a mere shadow of what it had been at its destructive height. Now every yard of the long main street was visible as the afternoon sun beat down. Now there was no cover for the three men. Every step that they would take towards the saloon would be seen by the outlaws holed up inside the Longhorn.

The banker inhaled deeply and mustered every ounce of his courage.

'Come on. Let's get this over with,' White said, gripping the leather straps of two of the bags. 'We ain't got much time.'

The three men started out into the street. Then with two bags each they began the long journey towards the distant saloon.

14

Sly Potter was leaning on the top of the swing doors of the saloon as the three bankers emerged into the bright sunlight. The outlaw glanced across at his six companions and grinned.

'They're coming, boys,' Potter announced. 'Three of them toting two real heavy bags each.'

Bart Savage rose from his chair and walked across the bloodstained sawdust towards the grinning Potter. He looked out into the bright street and narrowed his eyes until he too saw the three bank workers.

Savage turned and looked at the seated woman. Martha White was flanked by two of the remaining gang members whilst the rest of the outlaws surrounded Savage's other prisoners, who were roped together.

'Reckon your man must love you real

deeply,' Savage said, his brutal eyes burning into the woman. 'Him and his two boys are carrying six big bags over here.'

Martha raised her head. 'Joshua is a good man. He would do anything for me.'

Savage walked back to her. 'Even rob his own bank just to save your life?'

Martha leaned against the hard-backed chair and glared up at Savage.

'You are an evil person. Joshua is ten times the man that you are. They'll hunt you down wherever you go after this. I hope they string you all up when they capture you.'

Bart Savage raised an eyebrow. 'They might just hang your Joshua when they find out that he willingly handed over their life savings just to save the life of his wife.'

Her expression altered.

She knew he was right.

The black-hearted leader of the outlaws was totally right when he said that the citizens of Sutter's Corner might hang her man when they found out that he had been so easily manipulated by Savage.

Many men are disliked because of the professions they choose, she thought. Bankers have more enemies than most. When the townsfolk eventually crawled out from their hiding-places and discovered that they had lost all of their money they would be angry. Angry men when multiplied became a mob.

Martha made as though to rise from her chair.

The hands of the two outlaws brutally forced her down again. Savage leaned over and looked into the woman's face.

'You ain't never lifted a finger and done a day's work in your whole life, have you?' the outlaw growled. 'My boys told me you had a servant. You ever answered your own door when someone has come knocking, woman? Have you?'

Martha could see the disgust in his hardened features.

'I am the wife of the banker. I have a position to uphold,' she replied huffily.

Bart Savage grinned and straightened up. He rested his wrists on his gun grips.

'Well, if we let you live you'll not be the wife of a banker any longer. You'll have to work them little pink hands of yours to the bone just to put food in that fat mouth of yours.'

She looked outraged.

'I don't understand,' she hissed angrily.

Savage chuckled, then yelled into her ear. 'When me and my boys are finished you'll be broke. Just like most of the other folks in this town. When a fat old woman ain't got any money she has to do some mighty unpleasant things to keep on living.'

Martha White swallowed hard.

Once again she knew he was right.

Savage swung on his heels and looked across at Reynolds, who was sipping whiskey from a bottle.

'I want you get all of the lanterns down from the walls, Griff. Fill a bucket with all of the coal-tar oil in them and keep it ready.'

'Right, Bart.' Reynolds did as he was instructed without question. He knew it did not pay to ask Savage what he intended doing, for that was something that riled the gang leader.

The amply proportioned woman was not so wise, though. She had no natural instincts when it came to self-preservation.

'What do you intend doing with a bucket of oil?' Martha asked the deadly outlaw leader.

Savage gritted his teeth and exhaled loudly. His dark eyes darted at the banker's wife, making her recoil on the hardbacked chair as though she had just confronted a rattlesnake.

'You'll find out soon enough.' Savage grinned. 'The whole town will find out soon enough.'

Before Mrs White could speak again she noticed Potter urging Savage to return to the swing doors. The outlaw was keenly observing something interesting out in the sand-strewn street.

Savage obliged and strode over to where his henchman was standing with his arms on top of the swing doors.

'What you see, Sly?' Savage asked.

Potter raised a hand and pointed a tobacco-stained digit.

'Look. They're nearly here, Bart.' Potter sniggered over the top of the doors. 'Look at them faces. They look like a bunch of ghosts.'

Savage squinted hard to where Potter was indicating. He nodded his head slowly as he watched the men battling against the stiff breeze and labouring with their hefty burden.

'They sure do, Sly. I seen me more colour on a damn church steeple.' Savage smiled.

'They look real scared and no mistake.' Potter chuckled.

'Like men walking to a hangman's noose,' Savage added.

'Is that Joshua?' Martha tried to rise to her feet again but once more the hands of the outlaws who flanked her pinned her shoulders down. 'Is Joshua coming? Is he? Is he?'

'Hush the hell up, woman,' the outlaw known as Chuck Saunders growled down at her.

Savage glanced at the two men who held his prized captive in check. He looked at the outlaws in turn and gave them their orders.

'Keep her planted, Chuck,' Savage said, then looked at the other equally dangerous outlaw. 'You get ready to help with the moneybags, Tom.'

Tom Barnes walked away from the seated woman and stood close to the swing doors as Savage and Potter opened them.

'When we get the money can we head on out, Bart?' Barnes asked. 'By my figuring we could be across the border drinking liquor with worms in it before midnight.'

Savage's eyes darted at the outlaw. 'My business ain't finished yet, Tom. I ain't killed that snot-nosed Johnny Mason yet.'

Barnes looked anxious. 'I heard tell that the Texas Rangers are in these parts, Bart. We don't wanna have a herd of them critters swarming over us before we got time to ride out of this stinking town.'

Barnes was lifted off his feet as the powerful hands of Savage grabbed the outlaw's collar and hauled him close. Savage snarled into Barnes's face.

'Ain't you listening, Tom? I got unfinished business with Johnny. We don't ride anywhere until I've killed that bastard. Savvy?'

Barnes blinked hard. 'I savvy, Bart.'

'Good.' Savage released his grip and returned his attention to the three bank men as they drew ever closer to the Longhorn.

They were indeed like three ghosts as they fearfully carried the heavy, cash-filled canvas bags down the centre of Main Street towards the saloon. The sun was bathing the battered wooden buildings in its unforgiving heat, yet the trio of men felt nothing but the terror that gripped their innards.

Joshua White and his tellers paused

on the boardwalk and stared into the saloon. The banker turned and looked at each of his men in turn.

'Thank you, men. Drop the bags and high-tail it.'

Both men did as they were told. They dropped their heavy burden, spun on their heels and ran. Before either of the tellers had managed to reach the middle of the street Bart Savage had drawn his .45 and fanned its hammer repeatedly into their backs.

Plumes of crimson spray exploded from both of the running men as bullets ripped right through them.

The banker watched in horror as his tellers arched and fell into the sand not twenty feet from where he stood. Once again Savage had demonstrated his deadly accuracy.

'Oh, sweet Lord,' White gasped, and turned towards the outstretched arm of the outlaw leader five feet from where he stood. The bullets had passed within inches of the banker as they sought and found their targets.

White stared in disbelief at the smoking Colt in the hand of the grinning Savage.

'That sure was good shooting, Bart,' Sly Potter said, chuckling.

Savage silently nodded in agreement, then pulled one of the swing doors towards him. He kept grinning at White in a strange fashion as he cast glances at the six well-stuffed canvas bags on the boardwalk next to the banker's feet.

'You made it with time to spare, Joshua,' Savage said in a low growl. 'Martha was fretting that you might decide to make a fight of it. I told her that all bankers are nothing more than greedy cowards.'

'You killed them in cold blood,' Joshua White exclaimed frantically, pointing at the dead bodies out in the street. 'You backshot two unarmed men in cold blood.'

'Reckon I did,' Savage sneered in a mocking tone. 'Ain't it just a crying shame, Joshua?'

Rage filled the banker. He dropped

the handles of the bags which he had carried from his bank to the Longhorn. He clenched both fists until his knuckles went white. He made as though to approach Savage, but the outlaw cocked the hammer again and aimed the smoking gun at the banker's head. White stopped in his tracks as the smoke curled from the gun barrels and encircled his head.

'I'd stop right there if'n I was you,' Savage warned. 'You see me fan my hammer, but how many times did I fan it?'

White was puzzled by the question. 'I don't understand.'

'Ask yourself this: did I shoot five or six times, Joshua?' Savage raised the gun until its barrel rested against the banker's temple. White winced as the hot metal burned his skin. 'If I squeeze this trigger will my gun fire or not?'

Every drop of the rage drained from the banker. He stepped back from the outlaw and trembled.

'I don't know. I didn't count how

many times you fired that weapon,' he stammered.

Bart Savage turned and aimed the gun at the banker's flustered wife. Before the banker could say anything Savage pulled on the trigger of the .45. The hammer clicked as it fell on a spent casing.

'Just ain't your day, is it, Joshua?' Savage looked at the banker again and grinned. 'That's the trouble with cowards like you. No guts.'

Fury again engulfed the banker. White defied his own terror and strode up to the deadly outlaw and glared into his eyes.

'Kill me, you coward,' he shouted.

'No! No!' the banker's wife screamed out as Saunders's hands pressed down on to her shoulders, keeping her firmly seated on the hardbacked chair. 'Don't kill him. Please spare him.'

For a few seconds Savage did nothing except look down into the little man's eyes. His grin grew wider and his hands reloaded his gun.

'You *have* got a little spunk, Joshua,' Savage said.

'Why don't you just kill me? I'm finished after this anyway,' White snarled sullenly.

Savage tilted his head, then calmly pulled a cigar from his vest pocket and placed it between his teeth. He produced a match as though by magic and ran a thumbnail across its tip. As the flame erupted on the splinter of wood in his hand Savage raised the match to his cigar and drew smoke into his lungs.

'Tom?' Savage said over his shoulder without averting his intense stare from the banker.

Barnes moved across the blood-covered sawdust. 'What, Bart?'

'Tie each of them money sacks to the spare horses,' Savage ordered. 'And keep your eyes out for when Johnny Mason shows.'

'Right.' Tom Barnes moved through the swing doors and started to do as he had been instructed. Savage glanced at Travis.

'Tie this feisty old man up next to his wife, Dave.'

Before White could utter another word Travis had grabbed him and dragged him across the room. The outlaw pushed him on to a chair next to his bewildered spouse.

'Thank you. Thank you,' Martha White said to the outlaw leader as Savage inhaled on his cigar.

'Don't go selling your soul to that devil, Martha,' White growled as Travis roped him firmly to the chair. 'There has to be a reason why we ain't dead yet. His stinking breed never does anything unless there's a profit in it for them.'

'Just like bankers, huh?' Travis spat into White's ear.

Bart Savage raised an eyebrow and looked at both his hostages as well as the last of the saloon's customers, who were also hogtied in a corner near the pile of dead bodies.

'He's right, woman,' Savage said to the banker's wife in a sickening drawl.

'You should never sell your soul to anyone. It never pays to lick the boots of your enemies.'

Martha White was utterly bemused by what was happening all around her. Her entire world had been ripped apart and she had no idea why.

'But you could have killed my Joshua the way you killed those boys out there in the street,' she said in a bewildered tone. 'You must have some humanity left in you.'

White shook his head at her total lack of understanding.

'Are you soft in the head? His kind ain't got any humanity in them, Martha,' White told her bitterly. 'He's up to something. Heed my words, woman. He's up to something and it ain't gonna be good.'

Savage holstered his gun and pulled the cigar from his lips. He grinned at them. It was a sickening grin such as only a madman could ever evince.

'Your husband is the smartest damn banker I've ever met, Martha,' he observed. 'I *am* up to something.'

Reynolds returned with a bucket half-full of coal-tar oil. The smell of the highly inflammable liquid was powerful.

'What you want me to do with this oil, Bart?'

The outlaw leader raised an eyebrow and sucked on the end of his cigar. The smoke filled his lungs as he smiled at the banker and his wife.

'Pour it over the happy couple, Griff,' Savage said. His cold eyes gazed at the glowing end of his cigar. 'Make sure they're doused in the stuff.'

Mrs White started to shriek in terror as Reynolds moved towards her and her husband. Her unblinking eyes watched as the outlaw obeyed his orders and poured the oil over them.

Savage stared straight at the banker as Reynolds emptied the last of the coal oil over White. The well-bound man felt the volatile oil stinging in his eyes.

'What are they doing this for, Joshua?' Martha screamed out as the fumes filled her nostrils and lungs.

'What's happening?'

White lowered his head in agony. He blinked but the pain grew more intense.

'They're gonna burn us, woman,' the banker yelled at the floor. 'What in tarnation do you think they're gonna do?'

Savage raised an eyebrow. 'Yep, he's a real smart banker.'

15

Gene Adams grabbed hold of the brake pole and stepped on to the stagecoach wheel. He raised himself up and looked into the concerned face of his toothless friend. The rancher curled a finger and Tomahawk leaned down to listen to whatever his friend was going to say.

'I want you to drive this coach into the outskirts of Sutter's Corner, you old buzzard,' Adams said. 'When you level the horses up at the end of the main street I want you to crack these leathers and then duck down into this box. Do you understand?'

Tomahawk screwed up his eyes and his tongue rotated around his whiskers.

'I'm a leetle bit confused, Gene boy. Do you want me to drive this stage or not?'

Adams shook his head. 'I sure do want you to drive this stage into town, but when you reach the livery stable at the end of the long main street I want you to hide down in the box. We gotta make them think that there ain't nobody driving this damn thing.'

'Why?'

'Well, I'd hate for you to end up shot to ribbons,' Adams said. 'Plus, I need a distraction so me and the boys can circle around to the back of the Longhorn.'

The old man's bushy eyebrows rose.

'Is that why you chose me for this job, Gene boy?' he asked. 'To let the rest of the young whippersnappers know that I'm the best darn distraction-maker and wagon driver on the Bar 10? Is that it?'

Adams tugged the jutting beard.

'Nope. I chose you 'coz you're the only one of my boys who'd fit in the damn driver's box without being seen, Tomahawk.'

Tomahawk looked at the rancher.

'Red could fit in here if'n you folded him.'

The rancher smiled. 'Remember to hide in the box before any of them outlaws see you, old-timer. When you hear the shooting start, get ready with that old hatchet of yours.'

The ancient cowboy watched as Adams stepped into his stirrup and mounted his chestnut mare. The rancher eased the tall animal close to the stagecoach and pointed a black-gloved finger at his pal.

'Give us a few minutes' start and then head on into town,' Adams instructed as he spurred.

Tomahawk watched as the five Bar 10 riders thundered through the shimmering heat haze towards Sutter's Corner. He then glanced down at the two men standing close to the stagecoach. The driver and the guard touched the brims of their hats at the wily old man who was clutching on to the reins.

'So we've gotta walk into town from here?' the driver asked.

'Yep, and I'd walk real slow if'n I was you, boys,' Tomahawk advised. 'I got me a feeling that a whole heap of folks are gonna end up dead before sundown.'

'Then we'll walk real slow.' The guard nodded.

Tomahawk released the brake pole and slapped the reins down across the backs of the six-horse team. The vehicle started to move slowly towards the town.

★ ★ ★

Tom Barnes had only just secured the last of the canvas moneybags to their horses when a sound drifted along the wide thoroughfare on the late-afternoon air.

It was a haunting sound that, for some reason, chilled the deadly outlaw to the bone. Barnes tightened the last knot of the rope against the wide girth of the saddle horse, then lowered his head and listened even harder.

The sound troubled Barnes.

He moved between the horses of the

dead gang members as gingerly as a man walking barefoot on broken glass. He stopped when he reached the animals' rumps and then stared through the sunlight around the eerily empty street.

Apart from the bodies of the two bank tellers and the dozen horses belonging to the Savage gang, the street was entirely empty. Barnes felt uneasy as the strange noise drifted again through the late-afternoon light.

He swallowed hard. Some men sensed when their luck was about to change and Tom Barnes was one of them. Every fibre of his being knew that something was about to happen. The sensation filled him with an overpowering urge to ride.

The storm had ended some time since and the blazing sun was setting, but Barnes sensed that there was now a far greater danger heading their way. The outlaw lowered his hands until they rested upon the grips of his holstered guns. His eyes darted along the main street in search of whatever it was that was making the unnerving sound.

It was a pointless exercise.

An icy chill traced his spine beneath his shirt and jacket. Yet he was sweating like a horse. Then he heard it again. He swung round and stared down towards the livery stable. The sun was getting lower with each beat of his pounding heart and was now behind the tall building. A black shadow grew longer and longer as it crept towards the saloon and the nervous outlaw. Blinding shafts of sunbeams tormented his eyes as they pierced the gaps in the walls of the livery.

'What the hell is making that damn noise?' he mumbled to himself as he tried to see.

Barnes tilted his head as the sound grew louder. Whatever was creating the eerie sound, it was getting closer, his senses told him.

Suddenly, behind him, the saloon's swing doors abruptly burst apart as Bart Savage marched out into the rays of the setting sun. Barnes swung, drew one of his guns and aimed at the outlaw leader.

'Sorry, Bart. You spooked me,' Barnes said with a sigh. He rammed his Colt back into its holster.

He returned his attention to the far end of the street.

The tall gang leader stepped down from the boardwalk and did not stop walking until he reached the side of the troubled Barnes. He glared at the man with some asperity.

'What the hell is wrong with you, Tom?' Savage demanded. 'You've been out here for ten minutes or more. How come you drew on me? What's wrong?'

Barnes placed a hand on his boss's shoulder. 'Listen to that, Bart.'

'Listen to what, Tom?' Savage growled. 'I can't hear nothing except these horses snorting.'

'Don't you hear it?' Barnes looked stunned. 'You gotta be able to hear it. It's like chains rattling off in the distance.'

'All I can hear is you gabbing like an

old mother hen, Tom,' Savage said. 'Least you managed to pack them bags on the horses. Any sign of Johnny Mason yet?'

Barnes shook his head. Then he cupped a hand next to his ear and nodded.

'I'm certain that I can hear chains rattling out there someplace, Bart. Chains clanging together like fury. Am I going loco?'

Savage cupped one of his own hands to his ear.

He was about to dismiss the idea that Barnes could hear the rattling of chains when he found that he too could hear them.

'You ain't loco, Tom,' Savage drawled. 'I hear them too.'

The expression on Barnes's face resembled that of the three bankers when they had approached the Longhorn less than thirty minutes earlier. It was pale and fearful.

'Something bad is coming this way, Bart,' Barnes said. He swallowed hard. 'What do you figure it is?'

Savage dragged one of his guns from

its holster and rested the barrel against his cheek thoughtfully.

'I ain't sure.'

Barnes shook his head. 'Why don't we just saddle up and head on out of this damn town, Bart. This place ain't lucky for us.'

'What you mean?' Savage asked. He continued straining to work out what was making the sound that was definitely coming nearer.

'We lost us a lot of boys today, Bart,' Barnes continued, as he too squinted hard in a vain attempt to see what was coming towards them. 'We ain't lost no boys in ten years and today we had our gang nearly cut in half by a fat old lawman. This place is bad luck and no mistake.'

Savage turned away from the sun. He rubbed his eyes.

'There ain't no such animal as bad luck. We make our own luck in this life,' he snarled.

'I'm for riding to the border now,' Barnes said defiantly. 'I got me the feeling we'll all end up as dead as them bank clerks yonder if we don't hightail it.'

'Not until I kill Johnny.'

'We don't even know for sure that Johnny Puma is the same galoot that killed our boys way back, Bart,' Barnes said.

'I know. I feel it in my guts.' Bart Savage marched back to the boardwalk and stepped on to it. The porch overhang shielded his eyes from the setting sun as he again attempted to see what was heading towards the town.

Tom Barnes hopped up on to the boards next to him. 'Listen to them chains rattling, Bart. That's gotta be spooks rising out of their damn graves. We're doomed if we stay here.'

'I got me a score to settle with Johnny,' Savage growled as he kept his gaze fixed towards the very end of the long main street. 'We ain't leaving until he shows.'

'What if Johnny don't show?' Barnes said. 'What if that rancher he works for has sent a message to the Rangers? They'll send an army here to get us.'

Savage suddenly smiled again as at long last he managed to see what was alarming his cohort. He grabbed the bandanna of the terrified outlaw, then pointed his gun.

'Spooks, huh?' Savage snarled as he jerked the bandanna violently. 'Look, Tom. Do you see it?'

'Well, doggone if it ain't a stage-coach,' Barnes said sheepishly. 'Who'd have thought it?'

'Who'd be dumb enough to reckon we were being visited by spooks?' Savage released his grip, cocked his gun hammer and nodded. 'I got me a feeling that our luck is still sweet, Tom. Stagecoaches sometimes have strong-boxes. Get the boys.'

'OK, Bart.' Barnes entered the saloon and gathered the others together. Only Chuck Saunders remained close to their roped prisoners as the rest of the gang checked their weaponry and joined Savage on the saloon boardwalk.

'What we gonna do, Bart?' Reynolds asked.

'When the stage draws level I want you boys to shoot the driver and guard off their high perch,' Savage said in a deathly drawl. 'If you see any passengers you can have yourselves some target practice with them as well.'

Each of the seven outlaws drew his six-shooter and pulled back on its hammer. They were ready to continue their slaughtering.

★   ★   ★

Gene Adams, Happy, Red and Chip steered their mounts through the back streets until they arrived at the rear of the Longhorn saloon. The Bar 10 cowboys dismounted, secured their horses and moved towards the saloon's outhouse.

'What's Johnny gonna do, Gene?' Happy asked when they reached the back wall of the saloon, close to its rickety door.

Adams gritted his teeth. 'I don't rightly know, boy.'

Red eased himself next to the tall rancher. 'What now, Gene?'

'I'm going in through this rear door with Chip,' Adams said. Chip North nodded. 'You and Happy will head on down the alleys on each side, Red.'

'When do we make our move, Gene?' Chip asked.

Adams narrowed his eyes. 'Not until we hear the stage out front, son. Then we make our move.'

'Where did Johnny go, Gene?' Red asked. He and the rest of them drew their guns in readiness. 'He was with us right up until we rode into the side streets and then he was gone.'

'Johnny ain't far away,' Adams replied.

★   ★   ★

The outlaws watched as the stagecoach cleared the long shadows and its six lathered-up horses trotted out into the bright sunlight.

'Hear it comes,' Travis said with a grin.

'Gonna be a damn turkey shoot, boys,' Sly Potter chuckled as he stood between Reynolds and Travis.

Bart Savage looked over the heads of the dozen saddle horses tethered at the long hitching rails. He stretched his lean frame to its full imposing height, then noticed something that none of the others had spotted.

The smile faded from his face.

'What the hell?' Savage gasped.

Griff Reynolds moved closer to Savage. 'What's wrong, Bart?'

Frantically Savage pointed with his .45 at the stagecoach as its team hauled the hefty coach down the middle of Sutter's Corner's main street.

'Open your damn eyes. Look at it. There ain't nobody up on the driver's board, boys,' he exclaimed. 'That stage is heading into town without a crew.'

Travis eased next to Savage. 'There has to be someone driving it, don't there? Stages can't drive themselves.'

'That one is,' Savage said grimly.

Barnes shook his head. 'It's being driven by a spook, boys. It ain't possible for a stagecoach with a six-horse team to steer itself.'

Savage eyed Barnes.

'Quit talking rubbish. If you keep ranting on like that I'll turn *you* into a damn spook, Tom. It'll only take one bullet through that skull of yours.'

Barnes shied away from the angry Savage.

Reynolds narrowed his eyes. 'Where the hell is the driver?'

'Maybe the crew got tangled up with a few Apaches,' Savage suggested. 'There's still a few of them making raids on both sides of the border.'

The stagecoach continued to travel precariously down the main street towards them. One by one the rest of the gang could see that Savage was correct.

There was no sign of anyone driving the stagecoach. None of the bemused onlookers could see Tomahawk curled up in the driver's box next to the guard's shotgun.

'What's going on?' Potter asked.

Savage had no answers. He signalled urgently to Travis. 'Stop that damn coach, Dave. If somebody is messing with us I wanna know who and why.'

Like an obedient hound Travis ran out into the street and grabbed the bridle of the nearest lead horse. He stopped the stagecoach and looked at the dust-caked vehicle. The rest of the gang rushed towards it.

Suddenly, as Savage reached the stagecoach and opened its carriage door Potter raised an arm and gestured to the end of the long street.

'Look, Bart,' Potter said fearfully.

Savage turned and looked to where the outlaw was pointing. To his utter surprise he saw the threatening silhouette of a lone horseman drawing rein close to the livery stable. The rider sat astride his mount with the sun at his back.

Johnny was obeying the instructions Adams had given him, adding to the confusion that the rancher had known would arise when a seemingly empty stagecoach arrived in town.

Fighting his overwhelming desire to ride straight at the outlaws who had killed his beloved sweetheart, and start shooting, Johnny held his mount in check and watched them. It was the hardest thing he had ever done.

'Who is that?' one of the outlaws asked.

'Is that him, Bart?' Reynolds wondered aloud. 'Is that Johnny Mason?'

'It can't be. He ain't riding a pinto pony,' Barnes answered.

Although their view of the mysterious horseman was dazzled by the rays of the setting sun behind his motionless form, Savage could sense that at last his prey had arrived. He brushed his men aside, and stood beside the stagecoach and growled.

'Pinto pony or no damn pinto pony, that's Johnny Mason OK, boys,' said Savage through gritted teeth. 'I can smell him from here.'

Another aroma greeted the nostrils of

both Adams and Chip as they moved cautiously into the saloon through the rear door. It was the disturbing scent of coal-tar oil. Both men knew that normally the stench of that fuel was contained within the bowls of lanterns and lamps. Their being able to smell the fumes so strongly meant only one thing: for some reason the highly inflammable liquid had been doused around the saloon.

The rancher and the cowboy made their way through the saloon's storeroom towards the open door, which led into the Longhorn's bar. As Sheriff Willis had done before them, both men paused close by the doorframe and weighed up the situation.

The sound of a distraught woman whimpering filled both men with trepidation.

Neither of the Bar 10 men knew how many of the deadly gang were in the saloon. They also had no idea how many of the saloon's customers were still alive.

'Who do you figure is doing all the crying, Gene?' Chip whispered.

'Whoever she is, we gotta save her, Chip boy,' Adams responded quietly. 'I ain't partial to hearing any female sobbing. It riles me.'

Both men looked at the wall far to their right. It was riddled with bullet holes.

Adams crouched and rested the barrel of one of his guns against the flaking paintwork of the door. The young Chip carefully removed his Stetson and then looked round the frame of the door.

The sight of the lifeless lawman in a pool of blood at the end of the bar counter chilled the cowboy. He pointed; the rancher tilted his head and also saw the sickening sight.

Adams had known the dead sheriff for half his life. To see Willis like that angered the rancher. He could barely contain the fury that rose within him. He placed a hand on the shoulder of the cowboy and then raised himself up. The rancher jerked his head in a silent instruction. They ran towards the bar counter with guns drawn.

The attention of Chuck Saunders was diverted from what was happening out in the street to the very end of the saloon. The outlaw twisted his body around and caught the briefest of glimpses of the two Bar 10 men as they approached the horseshoe-shaped bar.

With a speed few had ever bettered, Saunders slapped leather, drew one of his six-shooters from its holster and fanned its hammer repeatedly.

The acrid scent of gunsmoke filled the bar as red-hot lead streaked across the room in search of the outlaw's targets. Adams ducked beside the mahogany counter as the bullets ripped the wood apart around him.

He blasted a venomous reply with his .45.

Then another ear-splitting salvo of bullets came from the outlaw's gun. Adams was about to return fire again when he heard a choking cry beside him.

The rancher turned and saw Chip clutching his throat as scarlet gore sprayed from the hideous wound. Adams reached out as the young cowboy fell beside him.

'Chip?' Adams gasped in horror.

The cowboy did not reply. His life had ended.

Gene Adams rolled across the blood-soaked sawdust and saw Saunders drawing his other six-shooter. Before the outlaw had time to fire his weapon the rancher squeezed his own trigger. Chuck Saunders was punched off his feet by the powerful bullet and crashed on top of a card table. Glasses flew into the air and smashed all around the dead body.

As Adams got to his feet he saw the hogtied prisoners whom Savage and his gang had accumulated since their lethal arrival in Sutter's Corner. The rancher kept his gun aimed at the swing doors and moved swiftly towards the oil-drenched banker and his terrified wife.

'What was that?' a surprised Reynolds asked Savage as the echoing of the gunshots came from the saloon.

'Chuck's in trouble,' Potter exclaimed.

Bart Savage turned his head and waved his gun. 'Go help Chuck. I got me a feeling that Johnny didn't come to town on his lonesome, boys.'

The outlaws were racing back towards the Longhorn when Happy Summers appeared from one side of the saloon and started shooting at the approaching gunmen. As Potter and his cronies started to fan their gun hammers at the stout cowboy Red emerged from the opposite corner of the building.

In seconds the air was thick with gunsmoke.

As if he were taking no part in the bloody gun-battle, Bart Savage walked towards the lone horseman. It was as if he were deaf to everything apart from the avenging tune which filled his rancid mind.

'You gonna let me kill you, Johnny?' Savage yelled.

Johnny dismounted. He held his hands above his holstered gun grips and walked towards the outlaw, who was getting closer with each stride.

When both men were within range of one another they halted. Savage swiftly raised his arm and squeezed on his trigger. Johnny felt his right holster being ripped from his belt by the uncanny accuracy of the outlaw.

'Are you scared, Johnny?' Savage taunted. He rammed his smoking .45 into its holster and flexed his fingers. 'Do you figure you're as fast as me? I'm gonna kill you real slow for what you did to my brothers.'

Johnny had one gun left in the holster on his left hip. He swallowed hard and went for the weapon. But Savage drew faster than Johnny had ever seen anyone draw a gun. He watched as the cloud of smoke encircled Savage's gun barrel. The bullet tore the Colt from Johnny's hand and sent him spinning on his heels.

Johnny looked at the blood on his hand, then stared at the laughing outlaw.

'What you figuring on doing now, Savage?'

'I'm gonna fill you with lead, Johnny.' Savage cocked his gun hammer, held it at shoulder level and aimed at his defenceless target. 'Then when you're pleading with me for mercy I'll kill you.'

Johnny lowered his head. Both his matched .45s lay on the sand. He shook his head.

'Why'd you kill her?' he asked. 'Why'd you kill my gal?'

'Who?' Savage smiled madly. 'You gotta understand, Johnny. There have been so many I can't be expected to remember them all. Look on the bright side, she was probably no better than a two-dollar bargirl. I probably done you a favour.'

The words were like a red rag to a bull. Johnny screamed out in uncontrollable fury and ran towards Savage.

As the outlaw levelled his weapon

Tomahawk suddenly appeared on top of the stagecoach with his lethal Indian hatchet in his bony hand.

'Hey, Savage,' Tomahawk shouted at the outlaw. 'Are you figuring on dying about now?'

Startled, Bart Savage looked over his shoulder and saw the wily old man on the roof of the stagecoach. The outlaw turned and fired just as Tomahawk threw his ancient axe.

The tomahawk sounded like a swarm of hornets as it cut through the last rays of the dying sun. Savage did not know what hit him as the hatchet buried itself into his chest. He fell on to the sand just as Johnny reached him.

Johnny stared at the body in disbelief as Tomahawk clambered down from the stagecoach and ran to his young pal. His bony hands retrieved his weapon from the outlaw's chest.

'He's dead,' Johnny muttered. 'How come I don't feel nothing but sick inside?'

Tomahawk was about to join in the

fight outside the Longhorn when Gene Adams came flying through one of saloon's windows and finished the last of Savage's cohorts off with two well-aimed bullets.

'Looks like it's over, Johnny,' Tomahawk said.

The old-timer turned and blinked hard when he saw Johnny grab the reins of his horse and mount. The young horseman spurred and thundered out of town.

'Where you going, Johnny?' Tomahawk asked of the empty air.

Finale

The silver-haired rancher stood on the hillside surrounded by a blanket of bluebonnet flowers. He rammed the shovel into the freshly dug soil and exhaled sadly. Again he had buried one of his brave cowboys.

Gene Adams turned and walked back to where Tomahawk waited beside their mounts. The rancher plucked his black hat from his saddle horn and placed it on his head.

'Chip was a mighty fine young whippersnapper, Gene boy.' Tomahawk sighed heavily. 'Just like all of the other folks we've had to bury here.'

'Yeah, old-timer,' Adams said. 'Mighty fine.'

Both men mounted their horses. Adams gathered his reins in his gloved hands and sat staring sadly at the beautiful hillside.

Tomahawk swung his black gelding round and looked at his old friend long and hard. Eventually he managed to say the words which had been gnawing at his craw since their return to the Bar 10.

'You figure Johnny will ever come back here, Gene?' he asked. 'I never seen him act like that before. Johnny just got on that horse and spurred. I saved his bacon and he never even thanked me.'

Adams straightened up on his saddle and nodded his head slowly.

'Broken hearts can make a man real ornery.'

Tomahawk nodded. 'Will he come back?'

'Sure he will, Tomahawk,' the rancher replied. 'He just needs time to think. That Bart Savage critter reminded Johnny of the love he'd lost. That hurts a man real bad. He'll come back, though.'

'How can you be so sure?' Tomahawk queried.

Gene Lon Adams smiled and reached

out. He tugged the ancient cowboy's jutting-out beard.

'This is his home, Tomahawk.' The rancher turned his chestnut mare and tapped his spurs. 'Besides, his pinto pony is still in the barn and Johnny sure loves that horse. He'll return soon enough.'

Tomahawk spurred after his pal. 'I sure hope so.'

Dust rose from the hoofs of their mounts. It spiralled up into the cloudless blue sky as both riders headed back into the very heart of the Bar 10.

We do hope that you have enjoyed reading this large print book.

Did you know that all of our titles are available for purchase?

We publish a wide range of high quality large print books including:
Romances, Mysteries, Classics
General Fiction
Non Fiction and Westerns

Special interest titles available in large print are:
The Little Oxford Dictionary
Music Book, Song Book
Hymn Book, Service Book

Also available from us courtesy of Oxford University Press:
Young Readers' Dictionary
(large print edition)
Young Readers' Thesaurus
(large print edition)

For further information or a free brochure, please contact us at:
Ulverscroft Large Print Books Ltd.,
The Green, Bradgate Road, Anstey,
Leicester, LE7 7FU, England.
Tel: (00 44) **0116 236 4325**
Fax: (00 44) **0116 234 0205**

*Other titles in the
Linford Western Library:*

LEGEND OF THE DEAD MEN'S GOLD

I. J. Parnham

Ten years ago, the Helliton gang holed up in a stronghold with a stolen wagonload of gold. One year later, all of them were dead — fallen defending their hoard from other outlaws, and fighting amongst themselves. The last living gang member cursed the gold, saying that if he couldn't have it, nobody would. Or so the legend goes . . . Trip Kincaid had always been fascinated by the tale. His brother Oliver suspects it's the true reason behind his sudden disappearance — and is determined to find him . . .

SAM AND THE SHERIFF

Billy Hall

Sheriff Ned Garman patrols his jurisdiction with Justus, his horse of many colors, and Sam, his loyal and shaggy dog. Together, the three make a perfect team. When a herder from Lars Ingevold's sheep ranch is gunned down, Garman is straight on the trail of the culprit, and concludes that the killer tried to implicate the Shoshone Indians in the crime. But Ingevold, constantly squabbling with the neighbouring cattle ranch over grazing rights, suspects the I Bar W is responsible. It seems that somebody's aiming to spark a range war . . .